DREAMWORKS
ЭBELOW
TALES OF ARCADIA
FROM GUILLERMO DEL TORO

ARCADIA-CON

Written by Richard Ashley Hamilton
Based on characters from DreamWorks Tales of Arcadia series

Simon Spotlight
New York   London   Toronto   Sydney   New Delhi

SIMON SPOTLIGHT
An imprint of Simon & Schuster Children's Publishing Division
1230 Avenue of the Americas, New York, New York 10020
This Simon Spotlight paperback edition August 2019
DreamWorks Tales of Arcadia © 2019 DreamWorks Animation LLC. All Rights Reserved. All rights reserved, including the right of reproduction in whole or in part in any form. SIMON SPOTLIGHT and colophon are registered trademarks of Simon & Schuster, Inc. For information about special discounts for bulk purchases, please contact Simon & Schuster Special Sales at 1-866-506-1949 or business@simonandschuster.com.
Designed by Nick Sciacca
Manufactured in the United States of America 0719 OFF
10 9 8 7 6 5 4 3 2 1
ISBN 978-1-5344-3355-7 (hc)
ISBN 978-1-5344-3354-0 (pbk)
ISBN 978-1-5344-3356-4 (eBook)

CHEATING DEATH

This wasn't the first time the universe mistook Foo-Foo the Destroyer for dead.

No—long before the ambush at an intergalactic way station, the robotic, rabbitlike bounty hunter was a soldier-for-hire. Foo-Foo had been a rookie looking to make his mark, just like the powerful warriors he'd idolized since he was a kit. So, when the fearsome race known as the Kotok launched their invasion of planet Xerexes, Foo-Foo finally found his opportunity.

After bombing the distant world from space, the Kotok sent in Foo-Foo and his fellow mercenaries to assist in the ground assault. And once their troop transports set down on Xerexes's cratered surface, Foo-Foo understood why the planet was of such value to the brutal, saw-toothed Kotok. Despite the destruction their incursion had already wrought, it was still a beautiful world, brimming with natural resources. It was still—

"Glorious!" boomed a muscular figure bounding across the battlefield.

Foo-Foo's large metal ears perked in amazement. His mechanical eyes dilated wider. And in a reverential hush, he said, "It's him. It's Commander Vex!"

Varvatos Vex dialed his Serrator from blaster mode to spear mode. The handheld device formed a serrated staff of solid energy, which Vex used to bat away several incoming Kotoks. A fellow soldier of fortune had to yank the awestruck Foo-Foo into a trench before he was struck by the swatted creatures.

"Yes, a glorious death indeed!" Vex cackled, his four eyes shining wildly. "Varvatos Vex can think of no greater honor than to die in noble battle against a worthy adversary!"

Even more Kotoks advanced on Vex, but another figure dispatched them with her two-headed scythe. Foo-Foo instantly recognized her from the news feeds he'd rewatched over and over again in his childhood hutch. She was Zadra, Vex's top lieu-tenant. Zadra pulled the protective face mask off her mouth and said, "Permission to speak freely, Commander?"

"Granted."

"Death shall not come for you on this day."

"Then Varvatos Vex is both most thankful and deeply disappointed!" said Vex.

As he and Zadra shared a private smile, the tips of Foo-Foo's radar ears peeked out from behind the trench. He couldn't believe his luck, even as he ducked laser crossfire in the middle of a war zone.

I . . . I can't believe this is happening, thought Foo-Foo. *To be here, on the same planet, with Commander Vex and Lieutenant Zadra . . . This cannot be random. This . . . this must be fate.*

Yet Foo-Foo knew that Vex and Zadra were the vanguard of a much larger counterattack. Xerexes had benefited from the protection of the royal throne world, Akiridion-5, for hundreds of keltons. And now that the Kotok violated that protection, Foo-Foo figured it was only a matter of time before they drew the full wrath of Akiridion's unparalleled military, the Taylon Phalanx.

If I want to get their autographs, I'd better do it now, Foo-Foo thought.

The gears in his bionic feet sprang into action. As he jumped out of the trench and soared toward Vex and Zadra, Foo-Foo unsheathed a brilliant orange blade from its scabbard. A master of close-quarter combat, he expertly twirled the knife in his armored fingers. Foo-Foo couldn't wait to show his skills with a hard-light dagger to Commander Vex and Lieutenant Zadra—and then ask them to autograph it.

"On your six!" shouted another voice.

A clear, blue bubble-shield suddenly materialized between the two Akiridions' exposed backs and the knife-wielding Foo-Foo. His metal body bounced off the round barrier and ricocheted out of sight before Vex or Zadra could spot him. Vex's many eyes followed the beam that projected the bubble shield back to its point of origin.

The acrid smoke from the battlefield parted, and Queen Coranda of Akiridion-5 emerged from the haze, flanked by members of the Taylon Phalanx. She constructed another shield with her Serrator to deflect Kotok sniper fire from the mountains.

"Your Majesty!" cried Zadra. "We must get you to back to a secure location. I'll send out an extraction alert on my Pingpod."

She was about to press an oval-shaped device clipped to her, but Coranda stayed Zadra's arm with one of her own four hands. The queen then calmly said, "Stand down, Lieutenant. For far too long I have sent soldiers to put their cores on the line while I wait in the safety of a remote palace. I now fight by your side. Any injuries you suffer, I too shall suffer."

Coranda looked directly at Vex as she spoke those last words, causing Vex to avert his four eyes. At least that was how it looked to Foo-Foo as he clambered out of a crater several yards away.

"Now, onward!" Coranda said, rallying her soldiers. "For Xerexes! For Akiridion-5!"

"Wait!" Foo-Foo called after them. "That wasn't what it looked like! I'm not trying to hurt you! I'm a huge admirer of yours!"

But Vex and Zadra had already charged back into the fray with Coranda, their gleaming Serrators punching through wave after wave of Kotok invaders. They cleaved their way deep into enemy lines, avoiding photon blasts, land mines, and razor-sharp teeth. Explosions erupted around them, yet still the Akiridions fought.

And Foo-Foo fought to keep up with them, even as the other mercenaries struggled to keep him on their side of the conflict. Foo-Foo kicked them away with his hydraulic legs, then spotted his idols across the field of battle.

He watched Vex come to the aid of one of his own Taylon Phalanx commandos. The young recruit had gotten swept up in the frenzy of war, forgetting his training and firing his Serrator at anything that moved—even his own superior officers. The delirious cadet nearly shot Zadra before she flipped her lithe form out of the way.

Sadly, Vex had seen this kind of bloodlust overtake other inexperienced troops throughout his long military career. The commander cupped his hands around his mouth and barked, "Soldier! Stand down!"

Varvatos Vex shoved away another Kotok and wrestled the confused commando to the ground, prying the Serrator from his automatically twitching trigger finger. Vex pressed down with the full weight of his body and said, "Slow your breathing. Feel the ground under your back. Allow your heart to become so still, you doubt that it will ever beat again."

Foo-Foo watched as the overwhelmed Akiridion gradually stop struggling under Vex. Once he regained his faculties, the young soldier said, "F-forgive me, Commander Vex. I—I seem to have lost myself for a moment . . . until you brought me back."

"It was nothing," Foo-Foo overheard Vex say. "Just an old soldier's calming trick."

The metal-plated mercenary forgot all about the invasion and even the signatures he wanted on his dagger. More than anything, Foo-Foo desperately wanted to know more about this trick. But the screech of the Kotok hordes interrupted him before he could even approach Vex.

Queen Coranda blasted with her Serrator, and Zadra swung her scythe as they fell back to Vex's position. The trio became hopelessly outnumbered by a tightening ring of Kotoks.

"Do you *now* wish you were back in your palace, My Royal?" Vex asked with an edge.

"It is as I said before, Varvatos," replied Coranda. "I fight by your side."

Foo-Foo watched the queen and Vex trade a look of final understanding before a large shadow eclipsed the lot of them. A Taylon Striker now hovered overhead. Translucent proton cannons manifested on the vehicle's underside and fired upon the Kotoks and their mercenaries. The beastly invaders shrieked as the energy blasts sent them flying this way and that. A hatch on the Striker then opened and produced a series of floating circular panels that arranged itself into a set of stairs. King Fialkov descended halfway down the steps and said, "Honestly, Coranda. Sneaking off on your own? What kind of example will you set for our future children?"

Coranda smiled at her husband and said, "A fiercely independent one?"

Foo-Foo saw Fialkov motion with his four arms for Coranda, Vex, and Zadra to hurry up the stairs. The queen and king embraced, and Vex took another look at the field of battle. From this elevated vantage point, it seemed to Varvatos as if all Xerexes was now infested with Kotoks. Foo-Foo's ears picked up Fialkov's voice from afar. The king said to Vex, "Worry not, old friend. General Morando

8

reports great success on the southern and western fronts. The Kotoks gather here since they have no place left to go. Victory will be ours by the end of the delson. And after this maelstrom on Xerexes, Akiridion-5 shall never participate in another war."

A nearby artillery assault made the Taylon Striker suddenly veer to the side. Turbulence rocked the staircase, and Foo-Foo watched as Vex and Zadra caught their king and queen before they fell over the side. Varvatos then activated the staircase controls, retracting the steps—even as more Taylon Phalanx soldiers remained behind, fighting back the Kotok on Xerexes.

"Commander, we must go back!" Zadra cried. "We must rescue our comrades in arms!"

Vex looked at Zadra with a heavy expression, then turned away. He saw the king and queen, the two royals he had sworn to protect above all others. Their ship took on more fire.

"Varvatos Vex hears you, Zadra," he said, his voice thick. "No commander ever wishes to leave a soldier behind. But tough choices must be made in times of war."

His words sank into Zadra's mind, and the last

of the stairs began disappearing inside their vessel. Confronted with the last chance to meet his heroes, Foo-Foo made another terrific, turbine-powered jump. He reached the lowest step and clung onto it for dear life as the Taylon Striker ascended. Foo-Foo imagined just how impressed Commander Vex and Lieutenant Zadra would be by his tenacity, not to mention his encyclopedic knowledge of their many exploits. The rabbitlike creature smiled under his helmet, mentally rehearsing all the charming, witty things he'd say to them—when the last stair evaporated in his grasp.

Foo-Foo pawed at the air as he fell. Before he hit the ground, Foo-Foo saw the ship's hatch close, sealing Vex and the conflicted Zadra inside with their king and queen. The Taylon Striker launched into the stars, and Foo-Foo's reinforced armor collided with the terrain.

His ears drooped in disappointment—then shot upright in fear. Legions of Kotok surrounded the lone soldier-of-fortune who had abandoned his post. Foo-Foo tightened his grip on the hard-light dagger. He counted the Kotoks sizing him up for the kill. There was no way he could fight his way free.

Foo-Foo abruptly clutched at his heart and

keeled over. His armored body hit the ground once more, twitched a couple of times, then stopped moving altogether. A pack of Kotoks looked at one another, their tails curling into question marks. They tentatively sniffed Foo-Foo's still figure, then held their pointed heads to his chest. Hearing nothing, not even the faintest heartbeat, the Kotoks brayed in disappointment. The pack let the tiny corpse be, and it set off in search of live game. And one full minute after it'd left him, Foo-Foo forced his heart to beat once more. Varvatos Vex's calming trick had worked again, and this became the first time the universe mistook Foo-Foo the Destroyer for dead. But it wasn't the last.

Foo-Foo shook the memories of cheating death from his head and took stock of his current predicament. He lay trapped behind the bar at an intergalactic way station, where one of the Zeron Brotherhood had tossed him—just as he'd hoped they would. Foo-Foo had marked the three other bounty hunters as soon as he walked into the nearly deserted bar. Of course the Zerons would be at this way station. They were after the same thing as Foo-Foo—the same thing everyone in the galaxy was talking about at the moment. The news feeds repeated the headline so much, he had it memorized by now.

"On Akiridion-5, a Coup Has Overthrown House Tarron. The Royal Family Are Presumed Dead."

Only Foo-Foo knew better. King Fialkov and Queen Coranda were goners. But their children, Aja and Krel Tarron, were still very much alive, as was their bodyguard—the one and only Varvatos Vex—who had only grown more legendary in Foo-Foo's mind since Xerexes's Maelstrom. He knew Vex would have piloted the royals' C-class mothership past this way station during their escape. If Foo-Foo could claim the reward on the young Tarrons' heads, it would bring him one step closer to finally meeting Vex. First, though, Foo-Foo would have to outwit his rivals in the Zeron Brotherhood—and fast.

"No witnesses," said the Zerons' leader.

Moving quickly, Foo-Foo ejected out of his armor and tucked his *real* body under the bar, behind a crate of empty bottles. The pleas for mercy from the bar's other two occupants—and the sound of the lasers that silenced them—masked most of

Foo-Foo's movements. His hidden body shivered in the cold, until he used Vex's calming trick once more to lull his heart to stillness. Omega Zeron stepped behind the bar and blasted Foo-Foo's vacant shell into oblivion. A quick sensor check then confirmed no signs of life in the vicinity. The members of the Zeron Brotherhood turned on their heels and wordlessly exited through the swinging doors.

And just as he did on Xerexes, Foo-Foo willed himself alive again. He scampered out the bar and headed for the docking bay. Slipping past the many busy transit operators, Foo-Foo stuck to the shadows and finally boarded his ship—a T-2 transporter with twin black-market turbo thrusters. He powered up the engines, donned a replacement suit of armor, and consulted his onboard navigation systems. The flight computer tracked the Zerons' path from the Oxiom galaxy to a remote planet designated as Earth.

These Brotherhood fools will lead me right to the bounty, thought Foo-Foo. *And my hero, Varvatos Vex.*

CHAPTER 1
INVADING YOUR HOMETOWN

"Great Galen!" roared Varvatos Vex. "Out of all the dark deeds Varvatos has carried out in his lifetime of brutal combat, this has to be the most core-crushing of all—clean-up duty!"

He hefted a refrigerator over his shoulder and carried it out of the yard and back into the kitchen. Vex returned the fridge to its rightful place, then looked at the rest of his Earth home. Usually, it appeared like any other dwelling in Arcadia Oaks. Little did Vex's foolish "who-man" neighbors suspected, an Akiridion mothership lay hidden beneath the façade of this midcentury modern.

But these were not usual circumstances. Vex's four eyes scanned the living room, still finding it in total disarray from the night before. Chairs remained overturned, shattered plates littered the counters, and several sharp knives stuck out from the floor—all courtesy of a recent attack from the bounty hunter, Halcon. Although the wall clock had been smashed during their tussle, Vex still felt time ticking away. Each new day in hiding on this mudball planet seemed to bring even more enemies after Varvatos Vex and the young royals under his care. Looking out a cracked window, he saw how the single sun was starting to set.

"Where are Aja and Krel, anyway?" Vex asked. "They should've returned from their education barracks a horvath ago!"

"You can ask them yourself," responded the mothership, her cool voice coming from the ceiling. "Our royals are walking up to the porch right now."

The front door opened, and in skipped Aja and Krel Tarron. Each of the human-looking teens smiled at the small plastic card in their hands, ignoring the mess around them. Vex cocked a few eyebrows at them and said, "What kept you so long? The solar cycle is nearly at an end!"

"Sorry, Varvatos," said Krel. "Interim principal, Señor Uhl kept us after school."

"To give us these!" Aja said.

She showed Vex the card in her hand, which featured a small photo of Aja and the words "Arcadia Oaks High."

"Official student IDs!" said Aja. "Aren't they lively?"

"'Eye-dees'?" Vex repeated. "What do these badges have to do with your visual receptors? Did a teacher see your true eyes through your disguises? I will bash that Uhl like a skelteg—"

"No, no, no!" Krel said. "It's short for 'identification.' It means our cover is working."

"We're all passing as normal humans!" added Aja with a grin.

No sooner did Aja and Krel finish speaking than their transduction effects wore off. Their human bodies fizzled away in a wash of blue energy, revealing their actual, four-armed Akiridion selves. Each royal glowed from within, the energies from their life-cores radiating outward through their pale blue skin and white hair. Frustrated, Krel threw his hands into the air and said, "As long as we come back here every twelve hours. Ay-yi-yi . . ."

"Well, more arms mean more help," said Vex.

"Consider it the next step in your warrior training, Aja. These are for you."

He thrust several brooms and trash cans into Aja's and Krel's numerous hands and pointed to the debris around the home. The siblings shared a disappointed look before loud barks filled the air. They looked down and saw their purple pet running between their feet.

"Luug!" Aja called over the barking. "How would you like to help us eliminate all traces of wreckage from our human household?"

Luug cocked his head, lifted his leg above an overstuffed garbage bag, and vaporized it with a squirt of laser pee. Krel leaned passed behind Aja and said, "That works!"

"Excellent," Vex said, nodding approvingly at Luug.

"What about the Blanks?" said Aja. "They are *supposed* to perform tasks like these."

"The Blank units masquerading as your who-man parents are otherwise indisposed," Vex said with an annoyed shake of his head. "They have been adding new data to their memory banks. What should be a simple task has turned into a simple disaster."

He pointed across the living room, where Ricky and Lucy Blank sat on a couch in front of the TV. Rather than get up and greet Aja and Krel, the two "parents" merely turned their heads around 180 degrees and smiled over their backs.

"Ahoy-hoy, kids!" said Ricky Blank. "How was school today?"

Lucy smiled unnaturally and said, "Anyone ask you to the spring sock hop-op-op-op?"

Aja and Krel took a step back from the malfunctioning Lucy. She stood up, walked backward to the kitchen, and spun her head around the right way, returning to what passed as normal for her.

"How about I fix a snack for everyone?" Lucy asked pleasantly.

"You know what they say," Ricky said. "An apple a day keeps the doctor away!"

Lucy opened her mouth as far as it could stretch and emitted a canned laugh track from an Earth sitcom. Vex covered his face with his hand, while Aja and Krel just stared at each other in confusion. Ricky then waved the royals over to the couch and said, "Say, kids, why don't you give the house chores a break? Come watch the boob tube with your old man!"

Aja and Krel shrugged and dropped their brooms on the floor with the rest of the clutter. They and Luug climbed onto the sofa with Ricky, but their smiles soon faded. The screen flickered from one station to the next at lightning-fast speed. The only one who didn't seem to mind was Ricky Blank, who kept grinning that rubbery grin of his.

"Uh, I don't think this is how you are supposed to do this," said Krel.

"Ordinarily, you would be correct, My Royal," said Mother from overhead. "But this Blank unit is restoring his memory banks with terrestrial tele-vised transmissions to replace what was lost during Halcon's home invasion. I believe the locals call it 'channel surfing.'"

Aja cheerfully stood on the couch, held out her arms as if balancing on a surfboard, and said, "In that case, hang a tent, dudes!"

Lucy Blank suddenly burst through one of the few undamaged walls in the house, carrying a tray loaded with cookies and a pitcher full of some bright-red liquid. Aja and Krel coughed and waved away the dust, while Vex snapped his broom in fury and staggered away.

"Look, kids—Mom made your favorite drink: high-fructose corn syrup punch!" said Lucy.

"We've never had that before in our lives," replied Krel.

Ricky Blank hooked an arm around Lucy and said, "Say, honey, that sure looks swell!"

"'Honey, that sure looks swell!'" Lucy repeated mechanically.

Ignoring the Blanks, Aja and Krel returned their attention to the TV. As a Food Magic 3000 info-mercial ended, Krel said, "At least the station isn't switching every second."

A new advertisement then began, broadcasting an image of thousands of humans in strange outfits gathered within some large structure. Aja, Krel, and Luug leaned closer.

"The wait is over, sci-fi and fantasy fans!" said the commercial's announcer. "The tenth annual Arcadia Oaks Comic-Con is invading your hometown—tomorrow!"

"'Comic-Con'?" whispered Krel.

"'Invading'?" whispered Aja.

The ad cut between footage of costumed people, boxes of comic books and toys for sale, and attractive humans signing photographs of themselves. Aja's and Krel's eyes went wide.

"This one has it all, Arcadia: Cosplay! Panels! Celebrity autographs! Gaming competitions! And any attendees who camp out in front of the Arcadia Oaks Convention Center overnight just might get a chance to see an advance screening of the newest *Gun Robot* film!"

Aja and Krel then watched a clip of a giant robot dueling with five colorful flying saucers in outer space. Their television vibrated from all the loud explosions and dazzling computer-generated special effects. The two royals gaped at the snippet of the *Gun Robot* movie for several seconds—before bursting with laughter.

"Is this meant to be a joke?" asked Aja between giggles. "There's no sound in space!"

"And those ludicrous star craft!" Krel chuckled. "As if any ship would have the subspace manifold on the *outside* of its hull! What a load of kleb!"

"I find nothing comical about this comic-con!" Aja said.

Krel laughed. "I agree! Who would possibly go to such a foolish gathering?"

CHAPTER 2
CRAZY TALK

"The Creepslayerz are going to Arcadia-Con!" said Steve Palchuk and Eli Pepperjack, high-fiving.

Steve sat in front of Eli's computer and resumed watching their favorite show, *Earth Invaders*. Eli watched over Steve's shoulder as the series's protagonist, Superagent Muldoon, wrestled with a tentacle-covered alien (well, an actor in a rubber alien suit). With a final punch, Muldoon defeated the squid-like extraterrestrial, and Eli went back to working at his desk. He glued some more bits of latex to a work-in-progress costume that looked exactly like the tentacle-covered alien from *Earth Invaders*.

"Oh, it doesn't get any more spectacular than this," said Eli. "Bingeing every season of our favorite show; telling spooky, creepy stories; and adding the finishing touches to our cosplay costume!"

Steve rolled his eyes, then saw that Eli was only detailing a single costume, not two. He paused the episode and asked, "Uh, Pepperbuddy, where's *my* suit?"

"This is your suit," said Eli. "And mine. The only way we can approximate the size of the Octopoid on *Earth Invaders* is for both of us to wear it together!"

"Are you out of your flipping *mind*?" yelled Steve.

Steve gripped Eli by his shoulders and said in a lower voice, "What if someone we know recognizes us in this stupid getup?"

"Steve, that's impossible," said Eli. "Arcadia-Con has tens of thousands of attendees every year. And most of them will be in cosplay costumes too. Nobody will figure out it's us under here."

A loud boom reverberated into Eli's bedroom, rattling the windows. Steve yelped and ducked behind Eli's bed, then yelped again when the ceiling thumped above him once more.

"That's it, Elijah Leslie Pepperjack!" shrieked Mrs. Pepperjack. "You're grounded!"

"But, Mom, that wasn't us!" Eli protested. "It came from outside."

He peered through the windowpanes and saw his front yard. Moonlight shone across the lawn and his mom's vegetable garden. The scene would have almost been serene—if all the dogs on the block hadn't been barking and all the car alarms hadn't been blaring. Eli looked up at the starry sky and said, "Y'know, Steve, the last time I saw something weird out of my window, it had stone for skin and—"

A giant rabbitlike creature suddenly hopped in front of the window. Eli fainted in front of Steve, who yelped yet again. Frantic now, Steve searched Eli's room for something—*anything*—that might help. He grabbed a glass of water from the nightstand and splashed some of it on Eli's face. The trick work, and Eli sputtered awake.

"What was it, Eli?" Steve asked in a hush. "What'd you *see*?"

"C-c-creeper!" Eli stammered. "But a new kind! It looked like a bunny. No! A robot. No! A robot bunny! With—"

Steve, having heard enough, splashed the rest of the water into Eli's face.

"That's crazy talk, Eli—even for you," said Steve.

As Eli wiped his glasses on his shirt, Steve

peered out the bedroom window. The dogs and the car alarms had stopped by now, and everything in the suburban neighborhood looked as boring as usual. Except some wild animal must have just devoured Mrs. Pepperjack's vegetable garden— all that remained were a couple of gnawed carrot stalks and a steaming pile of droppings. Steve wrinkled his nose and said, "Gross!"

From the shadows Foo-Foo the Destroyer watched the buffoonish blond life-form argue with the smaller, weaker life-form beside him.

Now that his belly was full, Foo-Foo resumed his hunt for the fugitive royals, Aja and Krel Tarron. He ejected a small mechanical drone from his armor and programmed it to search the area for unusual energy signatures. Like, say, from a set of Akiridion life-cores. . . .

Find the children, find the bodyguard, Foo-Foo thought in anticipation. *Commander Vex will be so proud of the way I've learned to imitate his every move that he'll forget the Tarrons ever existed. Varvatos will want to be my best friend—forever!*

CHAPTER 3
OTHER ASSORTED GEEKERY

"For the glory of Merlin, Daylight is mine to command!"

Despite the late hour, the Arcadia Oaks Woods filled with dazzling light as James "Jim" Lake Jr. spoke his incantation. Jim's Amulet levitated out of his hand and summoned the Daylight Armor, which snapped around his young body with tailored precision. A final pulse of energy surged down Jim's silvered arm and manifested the enchanted Daylight sword.

"I gotta say, Jimbo—that never gets old," enthused Tobias "Toby" Domzalski.

Jim smiled at his best friend, then at the other allies who stood beside him in the woods—Claire Nuñez and the good Trolls, Blinky and Aarghaumont, better known as AAARRRGGHH!!!

Claire smiled back at her boyfriend and said, "The councilwoman's daughter seconds that motion. I only wish everyone around here felt the same way!"

She activated a weapon of her own, the pronged Shadow Staff, just before the trees around them rustled. A squadron of Gumm-Gumms marched out from all directions, snapping branches and trampling bushes as they advanced on Jim and his teammates. AAARRRGGHH!!! growled at the evil Trolls, and the runes on his stone skin flared green, enhancing his strength. Blinky's six eyes bulged as he said, "Master Jim, I applaud your ruse to lead these Gumm-Gumms away from Arcadia and avoid the endangerment of innocents. Though I now wonder if we may have inadvertently endangered *ourselves* in the process!"

"To be honest, Blink, I didn't really think it through that far," Jim confessed.

"Aw, relax," said Toby. "We'll do what we always do in emergencies—smash things!"

"Works for me," grumbled AAARRRGGHH!!!

The muscular Troll charged full-bore at the Gumm-Gumms, who raised their Parlok spears. But at the last possible moment, Claire cast a shadow portal in front of AAARRRGGHH!!! with her staff. He disappeared into the black hole, startling the Gumm-Gumms. A split-second later, a second portal opened behind the evil Trolls, and AAARRRGGHH!!! rocketed through it. His momentum propelled him into the unsuspecting Gumm-Gumms, knocking them pell-mell into the nearby trees and boulders.

"Looks like our odds of survival—*Ngh!*—just got even!" Jim grunted as he deflected another Gumm-Gumm with his shield.

"Ha!" Blinky laughed. "'Odd,' 'even'—I love a good bit of wordplay, Master Jim. Almost as much as I love Dwärkstone!"

Blinky's four hands reached into his satchel and produced a quartet of Dwärkstone grenades. He lobbed the crystal bombs at the Gumm-Gumms racing toward him, and they exploded. As the smoke cleared, Jim ran his Daylight sword through two more Gumm-Gumms who were one in front of the other. The luminous blade pierced their armor and turned the evil Trolls into a pair of lifeless stone statues.

Jim then spotted the final three Gumm-Gumms retreating into the woods. He started to chase after them as Claire doubled over, coughing. Forgetting about the Gumm-Gumms, Jim, Toby, Blinky, and AAARRRGGHH!!! all rushed to Claire's aid. But she waved everyone away, saying, "I-I'm fine. Really. Been feeling way better ever since Jim's mom checked me out."

Jim knew his mom was a great physician. But not even Dr. Barbara Lake seemed capable of curing Claire's condition—whatever it was. Seeing the dark circles under his girlfriend's eyes only underscored just how exhausted and overburdened he and his friends now felt.

"Maybe we should head home," Jim said. "We're no use to anyone if we're too sick and tired to hunt Trolls."

"Master Jim, are you sure this course of action is wise?" asked Blinky.

Jim vanished his sword and said, "I don't know if *any* of my actions are ever wise, Blinky. But those Gumm-Gumms are running away from Arcadia, so no one's in any immediate danger. More important, I want to get Claire home as quickly as possible. She needs to rest." Claire gave Jim a grateful smile.

"But, Master Jim, the Gumm-Gumms—" Blinky began, but Jim interrupted him.

"Blinky, I think we deserve to take it easy *one* night this week. . . . Don't we?"

Blinky, AAARRRGGHH!!!, Toby, and Claire all shared a weary look. In truth, the past few days had been incredibly taxing. Yes, they had still managed to keep the existence of Trolls a secret from the humans in Arcadia Oaks. But Team Trollhunters also suffered the recent loss of their friend, Draal, who was now controlled body and soul by the ruthless leader of the Gumm-Gumms, Gunmar the Black. Even the thought of that monster made Jim feel as ill as Claire. The Trollhunter wondered how his many predecessors—like Kanjigar the Courageous and Deya the Deliverer—dealt with such loss when the Amulet was theirs to command.

"That's it!" said Toby with a snap of his fingers. "I've got just the thing to take everyone's minds off our current troubles—the Arcadia Oaks Comic-Con!"

Toby threw his hands into the air, expecting everyone else to cheer around him. But Team Trollhunters remained silent. Undeterred, Toby said, "Not only does this year's show have the usual mix of collectibles, memorabilia, and other assorted geekery, but it also boasts a lineup of special celebrity guests, including the cast of our favorite show, *Mistrial & Error: Swamp Law*!"

Blinky gasped out loud before covering his open mouth with all four hands. Recovering, he asked, "Tobias, do you mean to tell me that the actor who plays the noble yet unpredictable Detective Jim Belaya will be in attendance?"

"Are you *kidding*? He's got a whole panel dedicated just to him!" said Toby, pointing at the convention schedule on his phone.

Claire sniffled as she read over Toby's shoulder and said, "You know, this could actually be fun. They even have a *Murder House* maze!"

Jim heard Blinky and AAARRRGGHH!!! sigh, and asked, "Guys? What's the matter?"

"Alas, Master Jim, as much as Aarghaumont and I wish to attend this 'Comma-Con,' I fear our appearance precludes us from your human festival of punctuation," lamented Blinky.

"Well, first, Blink, it's *Comic*-Con," Jim said as he rubbed his chin, an idea forming. "And second, I think I may know a way to get you in there. . . ."

The remote-controlled drone hovered above the woods' tree line, just out of sight—but not out of earshot. Its audio sensors picked up everything Jim and the others had been discussing, just as its cameras recorded their brawl with the Gumm-Gumms. The picture and sound transmitted to Foo-Foo's mechanical suit, and he followed along from afar.

Hmm, three battle-ready human youths, plus two more life-forms from an unidentified Earth species, thought Foo-Foo. *Unusual energy signatures, to be sure—but these are most definitely not the Tarron runaways. Yet if these "Trollhunters" fancy themselves protectors of this planet, they may present a . . . complication in collecting my bounty. I cannot allow their potential interference to embarrass me in front of Varvatos!*

His then studied an aerial map. The drone's thermal imaging picked up heat signatures of the three surviving Gumm-Gumms as they fled through the woods. Foo-Foo's robotic eyes focused on the evil Trolls, while his suit triggered a playback of Jim saying "Looks like our odds of survival—*Ngh!*—just got even!"

CHAPTER 4
DON'T WAIT UP

Alarms rang. Voices screamed. And Aja Tarron's entire world fell apart.

She ran as fast as she could, cradling Luug in her four arms, while V-Strikers smashed through Akiridion-5's atmospheric shields. Aja dodged another cascade of neon sparks, hoping her brother, Mama, and Papa were somehow safe.

But the concern she felt only intensified as soon as Aja spotted someone else in immediate danger. A young Akiridion girl wandered alone through the decimated city block, calling out for her mother. Aja then looked up and saw another V-Striker tail-spin into a tall building right above the child. Aja tossed Luug out of harm's way and shouted, "Look out!" Then she started to run again.

She ran even faster than before, her freed arms swinging, her legs pumping like pistons. Aja was certain she'd be able to save the girl in time. Yet the tons of rubble landed just before she got within arm's reach. The child's cries stopped, and all Aja could hear were those alarms ringing, ringing, ringing.

Aja awoke with a start, her six limbs kicking off her sheets. She realized she was back in her bedroom in Arcadia Oaks, then looked over to the clock on her night table. The time was seven o'clock, and the alarm continued to blare until Aja hit the snooze button.

"Maybe I should try waking up to music again," she mumbled.

Krel walked past her open door, tinkering with another of his inventions. He noted the tense look on Aja's face and asked, "Rough night?"

"I was dreaming about home—to our last day on Akiridion. When General Morando launched his attack. It . . . it was *horrible*. . . ."

"I know, Aja, but we survived," said Krel as he sat on the corner of her bed. "And you were a hero. You saved that girl!"

"Davaros," Aja said absently, then remembering

the child from her nightmare. "But in my dream, I *didn't* save her. I *wasn't* fast enough. I wasn't a warrior. I wasn't the queen-in-waiting. I wasn't . . . *anything.*"

Krel wanted to say something reassuring to his sister, but the words didn't come. Instead, Krel's brain filled with complex schematics of a Daxial Array. Without the device or its components, the sole survivors of House Tarron would never be able to repair their ship; fly back to Akiridion-5; and reclaim their birthright from that traitor, Morando. Krel's and Aja's individual thoughts grew darker still, until Mother's voice trilled above them.

"Good morning, My Royals," said Mother. "Lucy Blank has prepared your breakfast. It's waiting for you on the kitchen counter. And the kitchen floor. And the kitchen ceiling."

"Ugh, Luug can have the floor food," groused Krel.

"And after your meal you may assist Commander Vex in repairing the damage Halcon caused to my exterior," added Mother.

Aja and Krel looked at each other in dread. After a full week of school at Arcadia Oaks High, the last thing either of them wanted to do on their weekend was more home renovations.

"Oh, ah, we'd love to, Mother," Aja began. "But unfortunately, we can't, because, um . . ."

"We have a, er, previous engagement!" Krel pitched in.

"Really? My onboard schedule shows no other commitments," said Mother.

"It's a late addition!" Aja fibbed. "We need to go to, ah, to . . ."

Just then, Ricky Blank strolled down the hall. In a singsong voice he said, "Need a little pizazz in your diet? Try the Food Magic 3000!"

Ricky then buzzed with the sound of TV static. It was like a channel changed in his head before he added, "Tonight on *Mistrial & Error: Swamp Law*, the Gator People file a continuance—for death! *Clonk-donk!*"

More static, then: "The wait is over, sci-fi and fantasy fans! The tenth annual Arcadia Oaks Comic-Con is invading your hometown—today!"

Aja and Krel both smiled and said: "We need to go to that thing!"

"But did you not refer to that Arcadia-Con as a 'foolish gathering' just last night?" Mother inquired.

"True! But we have reconsidered our position

as it may provide valuable, um, insight into fringe human customs!" Krel said.

Aja's eyes sparkled. "We are going to Arcadia-Con," she said. "Lively!"

The Tarron teens then sprang out of Aja's bed and ran past Ricky Blank and into the living room. They dove toward the fireplace, which opened like an air lock and admitted them into the mothership proper. Racing down polished metal corridors, Aja and Krel reached the transduction chamber and stood before a pulsing circle of light.

"Mother—humanize us!" commanded Aja.

"As you wish, My Royal Queen-in-Waiting," said Mother. "Commencing transduction."

In a flash Aja's and Krel's Akiridion bodies reconfigured into their human forms.

"Perhaps we should've asked Mother to prepare some of those peculiar costumes people wear to the Arcadia-Con?" Aja asked.

"Are you kidding? She can barely manage our regular human appearances," said Krel. "Look how short she makes my pants! Come on, let's get out of here."

"Wait," Aja said as she made toward the room next door. "Before we go . . ."

Krel followed her into the sterile stasis chamber, where Mother created replacement bodies for their parents' dormant life-cores. Vibrant yellow strands extended from each core, approximating all-new circulatory systems for King Fialkov and Queen Coranda. Krel checked the display beside him and saw that it would still be a couple more parsons before their parents' molecular codes would be fully rewritten. Aja ran her fingers along the transparent cocoons housing the cores and said, "Krel and I are going out for a bit, Mama and Papa. Don't wait up."

And from Mother's illuminated hallway, Varvatos Vex watched his two youthful charges bid farewell to the incapacitated king and queen. His shoulders sagged, as if weighted down by a terrible burden. Vex had grown to care deeply for Aja and Krel. He just didn't know how to tell them that—or that it was Varvatos Vex himself who was responsible for General Morando's attack on their parents. . . .

CHAPTER 5
INCOGNΞAT–O

"Lively!" shouted Aja as she zoomed on her hoverboard.

She had flown her board back on Akiridion-5, of course. But something about racing it around Arcadia Oaks made her feel more, well, alive. Maybe it was the way the sunlight warmed her skin. Or how the wind buffeted her blond hair whenever she accelerated. Aja looked over her shoulder to see if everyone else was having as much fun.

"Varvatos Vex has never been more miserable in his life," Vex said in his human guise of a curmudgeonly senior citizen.

Behind him, Luug—now in his Corgi form—let his tongue flap in the breeze, splattering Krel with copious amounts of dog drool.

"I am also having a very, very bad time," said Krel. "I don't know why you're so cheerful, Aja."

Aja ignored their complaints and powered forward. Fortunately, the housing development in which Mother had crash-landed was sparsely occupied. That meant she could really cut loose on the hoverboard without any nosy neighbors spotting her. Skirting around the town, Aja soon reached the vacant loading zone behind the Arcadia Oaks Convention Center.

"So this is the Arcadia-Con," said Aja as collapsed her board into a tiny disc. "What should we do first?"

"Duck!" shouted Vex.

He pushed Aja, Krel, and Luug out of the way an instant before a large town car swerved into the loading dock. The Akiridions formed bubble shields with their Serrators and bounced to safety while the sedan drove over the spot they had just occupied. With a loud rubber-on-asphalt screech, the car skidded to a halt, inches away from the Convention Center's wall. The driver's side door opened, and out stepped Nana Domzalski. She blinked behind her thick glasses and said, "Are you kids coming or what?"

Inside the sedan, Toby, Jim, Claire, Blinky, and AAARRRGGHH!!! were still reeling from Nana's dizzying driving. They kept their hands over their eyes, having completely missed the near collision—as well as the bubble shields.

"Uh, Tobes, not to sound ungrateful about our ride, but isn't Nana *legally blind*?" asked Jim.

"And hard of hearing!" said Toby. "But how could I *not* invite her? She loves Jim Belaya almost as much as Mr. Meow Meow PI!"

"Somehow, teleporting through a dimension of infinite darkness doesn't seem that dangerous anymore," said a shaken Claire.

"At least you lot had seat belts!" NotEnrique griped as his impish Changeling body tumbled out of the glove compartment.

Blinky and AAARRRGGHH!!! pulled large quilts over their heads to guard against any sunlight—and to roll their eyes in private. As they, Jim, Claire, and Toby staggered out of Nana's car, the unseen Akiridions dusted themselves off and left the loading dock. The young royals and Team Trollhunters passed each other without even a second glance.

As they got closer to the entrance, Aja squinted

her eyes. "At least the Arcadia-Con does not look as crowded as in that commercial," she said.

She, Krel, Vex, and Luug then rounded a corner and reached the front of the Convention Center—where thousands upon thousands of attendees waited in the longest line they had ever see on this or any other planet.

"Ah kleb," muttered Krel.

Inside the Convention Center a towering, tentacle-covered alien waddled forward in line, the top of its rubbery head snagging on an Arcadia-Con banner. And deep under all that foam and latex, Eli struggled to maintain his balance—and carry Steve on his shoulders. The heat was unbearable inside their costume, making Eli sweat more than he ever had in Coach Lawrence's gym class.

"Uh, Steve? Maybe now would be a good time for us to switch places?" suggested Eli. Steve just ignored him.

Eli looked through the peepholes he'd put into the Octopoid costume. Mary, Darci, and Shannon from school all walked by with VIP passes and said, "Hey, Eli! Hey, Steve!"

"What the *flip*?" Steve shouted inside the suit. "You said nobody would recognize us!"

Struggling to keep them both upright as Steve flailed around, Eli said, "I didn't think anyone could! Our cosplay costumes are so show-accurate, I thought for sure we'd be incognito!"

"There's nothing neat-o about any of this, Pepperjerk!" moaned Steve. Then he sighed. "Okay. Let's switch places," he said.

Farther back in line a uniformed guard skeptically eyed Aja, Krel, Vex, and Luug by the security checkpoint. Other attendees groaned impatiently behind them, eager to get through the bag inspections and into Arcadia-Con already. Vex waved his cane at the guard and said, "Varvatos Vex demands that you let the Tarron royals pass at once, or this geezer shall wreak a vengeance that is most swift and most severe!"

"Pleeeaaase?" Aja asked sweetly.

"Uh-huh," said the bored guard. "Well, I'm afraid I can't do that for three reasons. One, our Convention Center is a pet-free zone."

He pointed down, where Luug happily dragged

his butt along the Convention Center's floor.

"Two, your props are setting off our metal detectors."

The guard waved his scanning wand over Aja, Krel, and Vex's Serrators, setting off several high-pitched beeps and squelches.

"This violates the conventions strict no-weapons policy. Three—and most important—none of you have badges. Everybody needs one to be admitted into the convention. And unfortunately, we're all sold out, so if you could please step aside and let the *real* Arcadia-Con fans enter—"

"One secton, please," said Krel, turning away and typing furiously on his cell.

"Ooh! I shall play the telephone holding music while we wait!" offered Aja. "Doo, doo-doo, doop-de-doo."

As the guard gaped and the entry line grumbled even louder, Krel slipped an Akiridion optimizer onto the back of his cell. The screen suddenly filled with streaming columns of code. Someone dressed like the Green Laser Ninja noticed Krel's obvious lack of a costume and said, "What are you supposed to be?"

"A Latino," answered Krel. "Now stop distracting me. I'm hacking into their servers. And Mother's savings account."

"Do-dah-de-de-de-deep-doo-doo-dah!" continued Aja. "This is fun!"

"Please to check your manifest one more time, underpaid temporary crowd-control official," Krel said.

The guard glowered at Krel before consulting the guest list on his tablet. His eyes bulged, and he said, "There they are. Three tickets under the name Tarron, purchased with a secure payment transfer from Mother Bank. Whatever *that* is. I, uh, I'm sorry for the confusion, folks. Please leave your props here at security and register your doggie in the service animals area."

"Doop-doop-dah—Oh no!" said Aja. "Don't worry, Luug, we'll only be apart for a little while. After all, we must return to Mother before our transduction effect wears off!"

The guard shook his head in extreme irritation and said, "Y'know, that isn't even *close* to the weirdest thing I've heard at Arcadia-Con. . . ."

CHAPTER 6

SEARCH PARTY ANIMAL

The three Gumm-Gumms took another peek outside of their cave. Golden rays of sunlight filtered through the trees, inching closer and closer to their impromptu shelter. They had not made it back to the Horngazel portal in time last night and remained stranded on the surface world ever since. But truth be told, the Gumm-Gumms were in no hurry to return to Trollmarket and report their failure to Gunmar.

"Maybe we should head back home," said someone nearby.

The Gumm-Gumms instantly recognized the speaker's voice. It belonged to the accursed human Trollhunter they had been sent to kill. Hopeful that they might still avoid Gunmar's wrath, the evil Trolls grabbed their Parlok spears and filed out of the cave.

They stuck to the shadows provided by the woods, sidestepping the widening pools of sunlight.

"Those Gumm-Gumms are running away from Arcadia," said the Trollhunter's voice, closer now.

The Gumm-Gumms leaped over a boulder, ready to strike. But when they landed in the clearing on the other side, they found no Trollhunter. Instead, the confused trio saw what appeared to be some sort of metallic surface animal. It was suspended from a tall oak tree by a noose tethered to its large foot. The Gumm-Gumms took a step forward to investigate, and three more nooses sprang up from the fallen leaves. The traps snared around their ankles, and a hidden pulley hoisted them upward while simultaneously lowering Foo-Foo to the forest floor. The Parlok spears fell out of the Gumm-Gumms' hands as they swung helplessly.

Foo-Foo unsheathed his hard-light dagger. He then tapped a button on his armor, triggering another audio recording of Jim's voice.

"No one's in any immediate danger."

The Gumm-Gumms squirmed at the sight of the searing weapon. They pleaded with Foo-Foo as they swung pathetically from the oak's branches, but their Trollspeak sounded like gibberish to his ears. With the tap of another button, he popped open a hatch on the back of his suit and pulled out a bolt of white fabric. Foo-Foo tore the futuristic-looking material into three pieces, then stretched each out to ten times its original size.

"These spare light-sails for my cruiser will shield you from your natural weakness," he said to the dangling Gumm-Gumms in his modulated monotone. "In return you will submit to me and lend some much-needed muscle to my search party."

Foo-Foo didn't even wait for the Gumm-Gumms to agree. He detached three coin-sized discs from his wrist guard and threw them skyward. The discs magnetically adhered to the Trolls' armor and unspooled countless feet of circuitry. The filaments formed a web around each Gumm-Gumm, and their bodies stopped struggling.

Hopping high into the air, Foo-Foo slashed the nooses with his dagger. The Gumm-Gumms fell to the earth and kneeled, already under the thrall of his neural control discs.

Now I'm just like Varvatos, thought Foo-Foo. *Now I command a phalanx of my own!*

CHAPTER 7

SCI-FI-YI-YI

Three VIP Arcadia-Con badges hung from lanyards around Aja's, Krel's, and Vex's necks as they entered Arcadia-Con. The chattering voices of tens of thousands of other attendees bounced off the windowless concrete walls. Aisles upon aisles of vendors offered everything from vintage toys to sketching artists to rare comics encased in plastic slabs. The Akiridions' senses quickly became assaulted by an overwhelming barrage of sights and sounds.

Aja startled as some adults snuck into an autograph line beside her, rudely cutting in front of dozens of patient fans. She noticed how the line-crashers ignored the steady stream of exasperated grunts and sighs coming from behind them, then asked, "Is this a normal protocol for the Arcadia-Con? At school the students frown upon such behavior. On more than one occasion, I have been told 'No cuts, no butts, no dirty coconuts.'"

"It's a small wonder this species hasn't obliterated itself by now," said Vex, his artificial face creasing even further with dismay.

Two die-hard fanboys got into an argument in front of him and began shoving. One pushed the other into a pegboard lined with bagged-and-boarded Golden Age comics and said, "Nuh-uh! Deathblade would totally win in a fight against Snipersnake!"

"As if!" shouted the second fanboy. "Snipersnake is the superior intellect! Deathblade would be the loser!"

The fanboys tackled each other. Vex lifted his cane so they could roll under it, and said, "As near as Varvatos can tell, *all* who-mans are losers. Especially in this *inglorious* place!"

Krel paid only partial attention to Vex. A cute, bobble-headed figurine in a nearby booth had captured his attention. He was about to ask its price when a small boy beat Krel to it.

"Excuse me," said the boy in an innocent, angelic voice. "I was wondering, how much is that toy?"

"That's not a toy!" barked the booth's exhibitor. "That's a limited-edition vinyl figurine!"

The boy's lip quivered before he burst into tears. He ran past Krel to his parents, pointed back to the exhibitor, and cried, "That bad man scared me!"

"Ay-yi-yi," muttered Krel as another fistfight broke out at the vinyl figurine booth.

"I do not think I like this Arcadia-Con," Aja said.

"This is not a celebration of subcultures—it's a marketplace of misery and madness!" roared Vex. "Varvatos Vex hereby vows to smite these pathetic, obsessive who-mans and—"

"Ha! My knight does critical damage to your elf-mage!" someone shouted nearby.

Varvatos arched an eyebrow and peered around the corner, where several teenagers gathered in a gaming pavilion. They haggled over an ornate game board and rows of miniature figurines. Vex pushed aside one of the kids and said, "What manner of chess club is this? Varvatos Vex has never seen another of its kind on this world. . . ."

The teens looked up at Vex with blank expressions on their pimply faces. One of them said in a nasal voice, "This isn't a chess match, mister. It's a

Mazes and Monsters tournament."

"Mazes . . . and . . . Monsters? Tell Varvatos more!" demanded Vex.

"Well, it's your standard deck-building game, based on the old tabletop version," said the teen. "You assemble a pile of character, kingdom, and artifact cards, then roll the thirteen-sided die to—"

"Thirteen different ways to die?!" Vex roared. "Glorious!"

"No, thirteen-sided *die*—like the singular form of 'dice,' y'know?" the teen said.

"No, Varvatos Vex *does not* know. But he would very much like to . . . ," said Vex as he rolled the thirteen-sided die in his wrinkled hand.

"Oh brother." Aja exhaled in exasperation.

She turned to the side, expecting Krel to be there. But he was gone.

"Oh, Brother?" Aja said in confusion.

She spotted Krel being pushed farther and farther away by tides of crisscrossing fans.

"Oh, Brother!" Aja called out.

Krel tried to wade through the fandom foot traffic, but the crush of bulky outfits and people stopping to take selfies made it impossible. Krel balled his fists and was about to yell when he heard electronic notes start to play in harmony.

"Is that . . . a sick beat? In Arcadia-Con?" Krel asked himself. "But how?"

Rather than fight the crowds, Krel gave in to them. He allowed the surge of attendees to carry him toward the music, and he was soon deposited at the far end of the show floor. There, gamers played against one another on consoles, tested out virtual reality simulations, and flocked around displays of upcoming titles—like one called *Go-Go Sushi: Spicy Tuna Dance Edition!*

Krel watched two kids move on stage, trying to keep up with the colorful tiles flashing in rhythm under their feet. His eyes studied the sequence of light patterns. And when one of the kids decided he'd had enough, Krel immediately filled his place. His sneakers squeaked and his hair swayed as he danced in perfect sync with the *Go-Go* groove. The crowd went nuts. Krel smiled at the adulation, which made him dance faster and faster. . . .

Across the show floor, Aja wandered the aisles alone. She walked past a gallery of movie posters featuring offensive stereotypes of aliens and felt even more alone. Just as Aja wondered if she should have stayed home and helped with Mother's repairs, she heard a familiar voice.

It was Stuart of Durio. "Greetings, My Royal Queen-in-Waiting!"

He waved at Aja from the other side of a booth, and his terry-cloth bathrobe didn't seem so out of place at the convention. Aja waved back and said, "Stuart! What brings you to the Arcadia-Con?"

"Oh, you know yer ol' pal, Stuart—always lookin' to make a deal!" he said.

Stuart gestured to a sign above his booth, which read RETRO REPLICAS GALORE. The tables around him displayed various reproductions of ray guns, laser swords, cursed rings, and robotic endoskeletons. Aja picked up a plastic Viking hammer and scratched her back with it.

"I use spare parts from my electronics shop to reproduce props from fantasy films and programs on the telly," said Stuart.

He then looked from side to side, leaned closer to Aja, and whispered conspiratorially, "Between you 'n' me, it brings in a nice chunk o' change, which I then invest into my taco truck. Avocados don't come cheap, you know!"

"I did not know that about avocados or that avocados even existed, and what are avocados?" asked Aja.

"Oh! I found something in the back of my shop as I prepped for Arcadia-Con. It made me think of you," Stuart suddenly remembered.

He rummaged through a cardboard box full of junk and fished out a single item. It was an oval, translucent accessory no larger than his palm, with a small clip affixed to its back. Aja took it and asked, "Is . . . is this from my home?"

"Right you are, Your Highness!" said Stuart. "That is *gen-u-ine* Akiridion tech. I sometimes come across random bits and bobs during my dealings with certain members of—well, some might call them the black market—but that's an unfair generalization. Anyway, the black market threw that in free of charge along with my shipment of Pooplorthian quark conductors. Nice guys, actually. Don't know why the black market gets such a bad name."

"But . . . what does it do?" asked Aja, caressing the piece.

"Nothin', I'm afraid," said Stuart. "It looks fairly

old. I'm sure the neutronic batteries in it are long dead. But if you want it, it's yours. On the house."

"Oh thank you, Stuart of Durio!" Aja exclaimed, reaching over the table to give him a big bear hug. "But before I put it on my house, I think I will hold it for a little while."

"As you wish, My Royal Queen-in-Waiting," Stuart said with a friendly smile.

He then attended to some other customers, who were inquiring about a pair of X-ray goggles that may or may not have been real. Aja grazed her fingertips along her obsolete oval, until a group of attendees in matching uniforms walked by her. She recognized their outfits from an old television show Ricky and Lucy liked to watch, *Star Quest*. It was about a team of explorers in tight clothing that flew in a miniature cardboard spaceship, or so Aja thought.

She then saw how these fans all wore *Star Quest* logo pins on their jumpsuits, right over their hearts. Shrugging, Aja clipped the Akiridion oval to her own shirt in a similar fashion and rejoined the chaotic Arcadia-Con.

CHAPTER 8

UNDER HER SLEEVE

Several thousand light-years away, Zadra adjusted her cowl to obscure more of her face. Her heels clicked faster on the illuminated walkways as she picked up speed, turning down several alleys in quick succession. The last thing Zadra wanted at the moment was to be seen—especially here.

She reached a nondescript door at the end of an alley and rapped on it with the ring covering her two knuckles. A narrow panel shot open, revealing four beady eyes. They all narrowed with suspicion, studying Zadra's ring from the other side of the door. Their owner finally said, "Where House Akraohm meets House Ventis . . ."

"We shall find House Tarron—and the future," recited Zadra, completing the call sign.

She heard the clangs of several deadbolts unlocking before the door opened. Zadra stepped into the rebel base and waited for the door to shut again before removing her cowl. The guard at the entrance saluted her, his Taylon Phalanx uniform tattered and torn. Zadra nodded back, then proceeded down an austere hallway. She stepped over snaking power cables and past crates of fuel cells, until she reached a war room filled with holographic battle plans.

"Zadra!" said Izita, an Akiridion who wore the coiled sigil of a healer on her forehead.

She excused herself from a group of fellow rebels and embraced Zadra. Izita finally let go of her companion and said, "Please take no offense, but I must ask for the sake of the Resistance—you weren't followed, were you?"

"I think we are beyond offense at this point, Izita," Zadra answered with a grin. "But no, I made sure to cover my tracks. Not that it was difficult. Val Morando and his army would rather engage in brutal force than subterfuge."

"Indeed," Izita said. "Even now, Morando's loyalist shock troops are storming Akiridion's

58

neighborhoods, quashing any uprisings before they start. I fear it's only a matter of time before they find this one in Adronis Quadrant."

"Then perhaps these will help," said Zadra.

She reached under her sleeve and pulled out a few Serrators and other small military supplies. Zadra laid them all out on one of the lit tables and added, "I know these aren't much, but I can smuggle only so many armaments from the loyalist lockers without being noticed. May they bolster the weapons cache of the Resistance."

"Leader Izita! Lieutenant Zadra! You must come at once!" called a rebel agent.

Zadra and Izita rushed across the war room. Several floating monitors—their screens as battered and cracked as the rest of the base—depicted vast star charts spanning the entirety of the known cosmos. The agent pointed to a bright marker flashing on one of the maps and said, "We've just received this signal from a remote galaxy. It's faint, but it's definitely Akiridion."

"That doesn't look like a standard communicator frequency," said Izita.

"It's not," Zadra said. "That's coming from an

old Pingpod. Listen, it's sending a distress alert."

"Commander Vex!" cried Izita. "He was once equipped with a Pingpod, as were all soldiers in the Taylon Phalanx. This signal could be coming from him! This could be the evidence we've been searching for—proof that Aja and Krel Tarron still live!"

Optimistic smiles spread from rebel to rebel. Yet Zadra remained unconvinced. She said, "I do not mean to extinguish hope, especially when it's in such short supply. But I was with Vex before he fled our planet with the king- and queen-in-waiting. None of them had a Pingpod."

The very thought of Vex made Zadra sneer. She had recently seen a recording that confirmed her former commander formed an alliance with General Morando. Zadra could not guess what would make Vex choose to be in league with so vile a despot. But the lieutenant intended to ask Vex—and condemn him to death for high treason—just as soon as she found him and the young royals.

Izita smiled serenely and said, "Then we must rely on faith over facts, dear Zadra. Aja and Krel are out there somewhere. I feel it in my core."

Izita turned to the rest of her agents and said,

"Have you identified this signal's point of origin?"

"Not yet," answered the agent. "Our current telemetry only provides a general location within a radius of one hundred light-years. To pinpoint the exact planet, we'd need a much more powerful communications array. But the only place on Akiridion with equipment like that is . . ."

"Morando's stronghold," finished Zadra.

The Resistance fighters' smiles faded, and Zadra felt a pang of remorse. Even Izita seemed uncharacteristically shaken by this setback. No one spoke for several moments, until Zadra said, "I . . . I can get it for you."

"Morando's communications array?" Izita replied incredulously. "I don't think that will fit under your sleeve quite so easily!"

"Let me worry about that," said Zadra. "I just need one of you to describe it to me, so I know what I'm looking for."

The rebels all traded blank looks before Izita said, "None of us have ever seen Morando's comms system."

"I would recognize it," said a small voice behind Zadra.

The lieutenant turned and found a girl, no older than ten, wearing glowing headphones around her neck. Izita kneeled beside the child and asked, "Are you certain, Davaros?"

"Mother, you know I am the top technologies apprentice at the academy," answered Davaros. "If it sends and receives messages, I can spot it."

Zadra saw Izita actually considering it and said, "Izita! This is your own daughter! I cannot guarantee her safety."

"With all due respect, Lieutenant, it was Aja Tarron who saved my life during the coup," Davaros responded. "If I can do something to now save *her*, I would consider it a great honor."

"Spoken like a true Resistance fighter," said Izita with a mixture of pride and worry. "And I can think of no safer place for my child than at your side, Zadra."

Zadra watched the rebels in the war room salute her and Davaros, their rings glinting. The gesture made the lieutenant recall her time on Xerexes once more. And deep in her core, Zadra did indeed feel hope—hope that this new mission would go better than the maelstrom. . . .

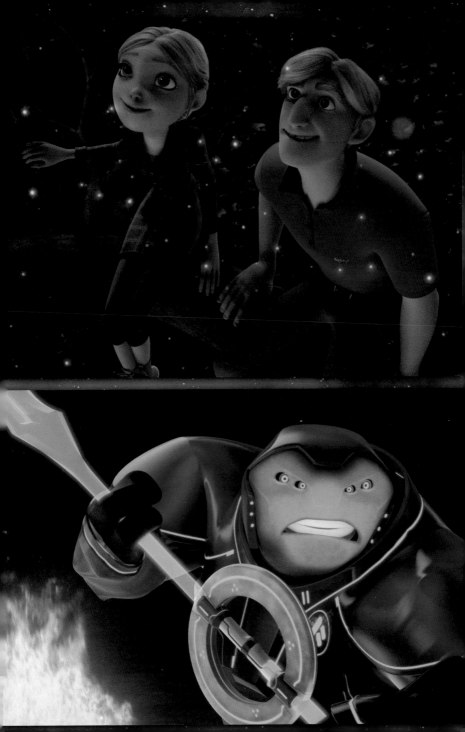

CHAPTER 9

STARSTRUCK

Clonk-donk!

The famous sound effect boomed through Arcadia-Con's hall A, causing thousands of fans to erupt in wild applause—including Team Trollhunters. Jim, Claire, Toby, and Nana leaped from their chairs in the enormous room as the *Mistrial & Error: Swamp Law* logo filled the screen on the front stage. Nana noticed the two figures still seated under her quilts and said, "Mr. Blinky! Arthur-San! Get off your duffs and join the party!"

"It's okay!" Jim whispered over the roar to Blinky and AAARRRGGHH!!! "Trust me!"

"Very well, Master Jim," Blinky said. "If you insist . . ."

"Here go nothing," grumbled AAARRRGGHH!!!, tossing aside the quilts.

For the first time in a very long time, Blinkous Galadrigal and Aarghaumont of the Krubera stood revealed in their Troll forms during waking hours on the surface world. And not a single human being cared. Blinky blinked his six eyes at AAARRRGGHH!!! in shock, then started cheering along with everyone else in hall A. One. A fellow attendee leaned over to the Trolls and said, "Killer costumes, peeps! What franchise are they from?"

Blinky and AAARRRGGHH!!! turned around, revealing the fake zippers Jim, Toby, and Claire had glued onto their backs before entering Arcadia-Con. Those zippers, along with the lack of daylight in the windowless Convention Center, gave the appearance that the Trolls were just two more humans in elaborate costumes. Stammering for a response, Blinky then said, "Why, thank you, er, *peep*! We hail from the, er, franchise of . . . of . . ."

"Um, *Tales*!" Claire volunteered.

"Uh, *Of*!" Toby added.

". . . *Arcadia*?" Jim finished uncertainly.

"Never heard of it," said the attendee. "But I

wanna get an awesome backpack just like hers!"

Claire looked over her shoulder, where NotEnrique clung onto her back like a knapsack. The little Changeling tried to keep his face still as he muttered, "This's humiliatin'. . . ."

"Hey, you're the one who didn't want a zipper on his back," reminded Claire.

"An' get it caught on me scruff?" NotEnrique said before pretending to be an inanimate object again.

The house lights in the hall went up as the *Mistrial & Error* cast appeared. The panel's host introduced them one by one to raucous applause. But the audience really went crazy when the actor who played the bayou-busting Detective Jim Belaya took the stage. Nana screamed so loud, Toby covered his ears and said, "Jeez, Nana! Now *I'm* gonna need hearing aids. . . ."

After forty-five minutes of behind-the-scenes anecdotes and teasers of upcoming episodes, the *Mistrial & Error* panel concluded. Nana rushed the stage with stunning speed, trailed by Team Trollhunters. She caught up to the show's star by the hall A exit and said, "Yoo-hoo! Detective Belaya!"

The handsome actor looked pleadingly to his

two handlers, but they just motioned for him to pose for a photo opportunity. He adopted a fake smile and said, "Hello there, young lady! Are you a *Mistrial & Error* fan?"

"Oh yes, Detective Belaya!" gushed Nana. "My grandson and I never miss an episode!"

The actor nodded distractedly and said, "Super! Well, I'm about to begin my appearance in the auto-graph area. So, if you could just wait in line and have your signing fee ready—"

"Why, certainly, detective!" swooned the star-struck Nana. "But I want to ask you about the Voodoo Priestess. Do you think the two of you will ever find love?"

The actor stared in bewilderment at Nana, who blindly followed him across Artists Alley, through the food court, and into the gaming pavilion—and got accidentally separated from Toby and the rest of Team Trollhunters along the way.

"Can it be?" roared a familiar voice.

Varvatos Vex stood abruptly at the Mazes and Monsters table. The thirteen-sided die slipped from his fingers as he saw Nana before him and sighed, *"Enchantress . . ."*

"Ooh, Varvatos!" Nana giggled. "I didn't realize you were also a devotee of pop culture!"

Vex surveyed the masquerading attendees around him and said, "Yes, Varvatos Vex would very much like to *pop* this so-called who-man culture—just as he popped the heads off the putrid pus-eels on Zebulon-12!"

"Uh-huh," said Nana, missing most of what Vex said. "Varvatos, I'd like you to meet my new friend, Detective Jim Belaya."

The helpless TV personality, who was hemmed in on all sides by the crowds, said, "Lady, I'm an actor! Belaya is just a character I play on—"

"Belaya!" interrupted a scowling Vex. "Stay your tongue, you insolent larvox, lest Varvatos Vex tears it from your gibbering skull!"

"My name is Marc!" screamed the actor. "Marc Scott Bradley!"

"Then those are the three words Varvatos Vex shall etch onto your tombstone!" Vex screamed back. "For the commander of the Taylon Phalanx now challenges you to a duel for the honor of fair Nana Domzalski—a death duel!"

The actor began to sweat as the teenagers in

a gaming tournament chanted, "Death duel! Death duel! Death duel!"

Their voices carried over to the *Go-Go Sushi: Spicy Tuna Dance Edition!* stage, where Krel was working up a sweat of his own. He had advanced to level twenty, drawing an audience almost as large as the one in hall A. But when he heard the chant, followed by Vex's mad cackle, Krel knew he needed to hit the pause button.

"Seklos and Galen," uttered Krel, who spotted Vex brandishing his cane like a club.

He hopped off the dance floor to the disappointment of the masses and hustled over to intercede at the gaming pavilion—only to bump into a group of vaguely familiar faces.

"Nice moves up there, Krel!" said one of them.

"Er, thank you . . . fellow students of Arcadia Oaks High School," Krel replied.

The princeling might not have been able to remember any of their names, but he certainly remembered their faces. These were the quiet kids he noticed in the school halls. The ones who kept to themselves, didn't speak up in class despite earning the best grades, and buried their noses in books during lunchtime.

"Now, if you will excuse me, I must prevent my legal guardian from bludgeoning another old person," said Krel.

He gave his normally reserved classmates a curt nod, then ran off toward Vex. The kids watched him go, and a few of them sighed "Wooooow!"

Krel completely missed their reactions—and completely missed Aja, who was similarly distracted by her surroundings. Costumes that had been worn by various actresses in various forms of entertainment genres appeared behind glass. The exhibit was entitled "Warrior Queens: Fashion in Fantasy." Aja's eyes studied the brocaded gowns of dragon princesses, the armored breastplates of Viking Valkyries, and the battle suits of postapocalyptic female freedom fighters. Reaching the end of the exhibit, Aja gasped at the most impressive figure of all—that of a space-age, time-traveling heroine, Sally-Go-Back. Kneeling in awe before the mannequin, Aja marveled at Sally's stylized ray gun and jet pack. The sight of such fabulous gear worn by such a strong, independent character filled Aja's core with inspiration—and a twinge of dread.

How do I ever live up to the examples set by

these human heroes? wondered Aja. *How can I become a warrior queen like Mama when I don't have the training, let alone a throne? Will I ever be a—*

"Ninja-kicking angel!" said a loud but muffled voice.

Aja screamed at the top of her lungs at the great, tentacled beast coming for her. She reached instinctively for her Serrator, only to remember she'd remanded it at the security checkpoint. The creature lurched closer and closer, its tendrils outstretched. Thinking fast, Aja recalled the self-defense move Vex had recently taught her. She jumped forward and planted a tremendous toe-kick right into the monstrosity's midsection. Aja heard two independent yelps before the tentacle thing spilled over and split open. Steve and Eli crawled out from the severed halves of their costume, wincing in pain.

"The blond oaf! And Snackbutt!" Aja said. "I thought you were a Zorkian cephaloplasmus!"

"I'll take that as a compliment, I guess . . . ," groaned Eli.

Steve wriggled out of the top end of the costume

and tried to play off the whole thing, saying, "Of course! I, uh, wanted you to think we were a, um, Zorkying shelf-a-pottomus! So, um, do you like my costume?"

"Hey!" cried Eli, massaging his bruised side and ego as Steve took all the credit.

Aja wiggled one of the limp tentacles and said, "Oh yes, it is very lively! Well, *was* very lively. Until I kicked it."

"Ha-ha-ha! Don't worry about it!" crowed Steve. "It didn't take long to make anyway!"

Eli glowered jealously and said, "Steve, we need to get going. Now."

"No, we don't, Pepperjoke," said Steve, his eyes still on Aja.

"Yes, we do," Eli insisted. "It was supposed to be a surprise, but I got us *these*."

He pulled out two crisp all-access Arcadia-Con passes. Steve's jaw dropped as he took one of the passes and read the fine print.

"No way! These'll get us backstage at the *Earth Invaders* panel!" Steve exclaimed.

"*Earth Invaders*?" exclaimed Aja, suddenly looking very self-conscious.

"We're gonna meet Superagent Muldoon!" Steve went on obliviously.

"Yes. Barring any other *distractions*," said Eli with a pointed look at Aja.

Steve looked from the passes to Aja and back again, wavering.

Aja smiled and said, "I should probably find my brother and geezer. I hope you and the Jack of Peppers enjoy the stage on your backs!"

Eli furrowed his brow in confusion at Aja. But Steve just winked, suavely pointed a finger, and made a clicking sound with his mouth.

"Catch ya around the Con!" said Steve as Eli dragged him and their costume away.

The metal detectors went wild as Foo-Foo passed under them, followed by his three cloaked Gumm-Gumms and drone. Normally, the bounty hunter preferred to avoid enclosed spaces. But his sensors had tracked the unique energy signatures of three and a half Akiridion life-cores to this very location.

The same security guard at the entrance hiked up his belt and said, "You'll have to surrender your props and submit to a full costume inspection, little fella."

"Foo-Foo the Destroyer submits to no man," said Foo-Foo in his monotone.

He flipped high over the guard, then kicked him in the back. The move sent the guard stumbling into the disguised Gumm-Gumms, who promptly tossed him outside. Nearby attendees clapped and snapped photos, mistaking the tossed guard for some live-action role-playing performance. Ignoring them, Foo-Foo pressed his wrist guard. The numerous traps he had previously planted around all the exits now activated. Impenetrable metal barriers fanned out of each device, blocking every single door and air vent into and out of the Convention Center.

"Lockdown initiated," said the bounty hunter. "The Tarron children hide somewhere among the rest of the riffraff."

Foo-Foo consulted his scanner once again, only to see the signal's reception fade in and out. He slapped the side of the scanner to little avail.

"It would appear this edifice's thick walls and primitive plumbing are generating interference," Foo-Foo said, then pointed to his drone. "Scan the area from above and neutralize any alien life-forms you encounter. The Zerons may have followed the royals here, as well."

The drone bowed in midair, and Foo-Foo then said to the Gumm-Gumms, "We know from last night's recording that the local protectors are also present. Locate and destroy these 'Trollhunters' while I find the renegade royals and the only being in the universe who could possibly understand me—Varvatos Vex!"

The Gumm-Gumms grunted in assent and marched off in one direction. The drone flew away in another. And Foo-Foo set off on a third. He hopped past the designated service animals center. Foo-Foo's sensors chimed, registering half an Akiridion energy signature again. But Luug backed into one of the metal kennel cages, and the sensors went blank once more.

"Blasted interference," muttered Foo-Foo before resuming his hunt.

Luug emerged from the cage. He paced back and forth, and growled at the armored rabbitlike creature, sensing the danger posed by Foo-Foo, but unable to do anything about it. . . .

CHAPTER 10

HASHTAG MURDER

Shrieks of terror reverberated throughout Arcadia-Con. Attendees ran screaming out of the *Murder House* maze erected in the middle of the convention—and right past Team Trollhunters. AAARRRGGHH!!! winced at the loud, giddy noise, and Blinky said, "Choosing to become frightened *on purpose*. . . . What an odd human custom!"

"I know it seems strange, Blinky," Claire said. "But seeing a scary movie can sometimes help people take their minds off everyday problems."

"Belaya!" roared an old man's voice from far away.

"Whoa," said Toby. "Someone's a bigger *Mistrial & Error* fan than we are!"

"A bigger *glork*, is more like it!" cracked NotEnrique from Claire's back.

Blinky considered the attraction's entrance, which resembled a dilapidated old house, and said, "What horrors can we expect to encounter in this labyrinth of lurking abominations?"

"Whatever it is, it can't be as bad as Toby's puns!" Jim joked.

He and Toby playfully elbowed each other while their group entered the maze. They were soon greeted by paid actors in undead-construction-worker makeup, who jumped from the shadows. The Trollhunters merely stared at the zombie builders, unfazed by their theatrics.

The group rounded a corner in the maze, then another, quickly getting lost in the turns and film-accurate details. Claire pointed in excitement at all the sentient drills, table saws, and belt sanders whirring on their own and said, "Look! It's the possessed power tools from *Murder House 6: Renovated for Evil*!"

"And the psychic interior decorator from part nine, *Twilight Zoning Permits*!" said Jim.

Blinky then saw three bodies draped in white sheets and said, "What manner of spectral beings are these supposed to be?"

"I dunno," said Toby as he inspected the trio up close. "Bedsheet ghosts aren't part of the established *Murder House* lore. So, either the production company cheaped out on this part of the maze or this is the laziest cosplay costume I've ever seen!"

Dry-ice smoke blew into the corridor, and AAARRRGGHH!!!'s keen Krubera nose detected a new scent in the breeze. He snarled and yanked the fabric off the figures, revealing three Gumm-Gumms. Claire noticed their circuitry-laced bodies and said, "Anyone else think they look a little high-tech for Trolls?"

Jim reached for his Amulet, just as Toby and Claire reached for their collapsed weapons. But before they could activate them, three new bodies intruded on the scene. Mary, Darci, and Shannon all huddled together in mock fear as they tiptoed through the maze. Team Trollhunters hastily hid their gear.

"Oh, uh, hey, Darci!" Toby said. "I thought you said you weren't into comic-cons!"

"I wasn't, Toby-Pie!" said Darci. "But Shannon won these tickets on a radio giveaway!"

The mindless Gumm-Gumms appeared equally

unsure of their next move. Foo-Foo's orders played in a loop in their heads—*Locate and destroy these 'Trollhunters.' . . . Locate and destroy these 'Trollhunters'*—but he had given no instructions about innocent bystanders.

Mary flashed a peace sign and took a selfie in front of the startled Gumm-Gumms. Mary then posted the picture to her social media, reading aloud what she was typing. "Hashtag Arcadia-Con, hashtag *Murder House*, hashtag lame monster suits!"

The hardwired Gumm-Gumms shambled forward. Mary, Darci, and Shannon tittered in delight. But Jim and the others sprang into action, knowing this was no game.

"We need to get Mary, Darci, and Shannon clear of these Gumm-Gumms," whispered Claire.

"But without the use of any special abilities, lest you expose Trollkind's existence to your gossip-spewing peers!" whispered Blinky.

"I know!" Jim whispered back. "So what's the plan, Jimbo?" whispered Toby.

"I DON'T KNOW!" Jim yelped as he dodged a Parlok spear.

"'*Goblins and ghoulies and things that go boo, we will pound into goo, we are coming for you*'— take it away, Steve!"

Eli waited for Steve to sing the next verse. But Steve merely gazed out at Arcadia-Con with a dreamy, faraway look. Annoyed, Eli dropped their Octopoid cosplay costume in front of the *Earth Invaders* VIP lounge. To prompt Steve, he then added, "'*Friendship forever will stop all the Creepers. We know all the secrets, for we are the keepers of—*'"

"Aja," Steve said absentmindedly.

"Ste-eve!" Eli whined. "That isn't part of our Creepslayerz theme song!"

He hauled their rubber squid alien cosplay costume up to a bodyguard stationed at the VIP entrance and flashed the two backstage passes. The bodyguard unhooked the velvet rope. Steve snapped out of his reverie long enough to see Eli stomp into the lounge.

"Whoa, wait!" Steve yelped.

He caught up with Eli inside the exclusive area and took in their swanky surroundings. Various film and TV industry types snacked on delicious hors d'oeuvres, relaxed in plush couches, and networked with free Wi-Fi. Eli screwed up his face in disgust and said, "Typical. Hollywood comes to a comic convention and makes it all about them!"

"Yeah, but aren't they also helping?" asked Steve. "By turning weird stories that dorks like you love into big-budget movies and stuff?"

"I see they've gotten to you, too," Eli said drily.

"But you're the one who wanted to come here in the first place!" snapped Steve.

"That's right!" Eli snapped back. "I pulled a *lot* of strings to get us in here! Just like I always do nice things for us! But do you ever reciprocate? No! You just take credit for my work before shoving me into a locker and talking to someone cooler! And making fun of my name!"

"No, I don't, Pepperjer—" Steve started, before catching himself. "I mean, *no, I don't.*"

Everyone in the lounge had heard Eli's raised voice and were staring at the arguing high schoolers. Feeling self-conscious, Steve jabbed his finger into Eli's chest and said, "Why don't you back off, Eli?"

Eli pushed away Steve's hand, then rubbed the sore spot where Steve had poked him. His eyes looked hurt behind his glasses, and he felt heat radiating from the back of his neck.

"I used to have a life of my own before the Creepslayerz were even a thing, y'know!" Steve went on. "I had interests! Sports, my Vespa, sports, some acting—sports! But now, you're trying to, like, *latch on to* everything I do! It feels like we're always together!"

"Oh *really*?" Eli yelled back.

By way of answer, Steve indicated the two broken halves of their shared cosplay costume and said, "*Really*. The Palchuk needs his space, Eli."

"Fine!" Eli said. "If it's space you want, Steve, then it's space you'll get!"

"Did someone say 'space'?" someone else asked behind them.

The Creepslayerz both froze in place. They *knew* that voice. They'd heard it season after season on their favorite program. Steve and Eli slowly turned around and saw the manly, chiseled face of the lead actor on *Earth Invaders*.

"Superagent Muldoon!" Steve and Eli said in unison.

"I see you guys are fans of the show. Thanks for watching!" said the actor, who then noticed their costume on the floor. "Hey! That looks just like the Octopoid I fought in season three!"

"I . . . we . . . you . . . costume . . . ," Steve blathered.

"We're cosplayerz," Eli filled in for his incoherent friend. "With a z."

The actor threw back his blond head and gave a hearty laugh, then pulled out a marker from his blazer pocket. He signed the latex suit—"To the Cosplayerz! Keep reaching for the stars!"—then bumped fists with Eli and the still-stunned Steve.

"Actually, sir, may I ask you a question about a season two storyline?" asked Eli.

"Sure thing! But first, I gotta ask this guy about his workout regimen!" the actor said to Steve. "It's almost like we use the same personal trainer! How much do you bench?"

"Is that before or after my daily workout of five hundred burpees?" Steve smirked.

"Didn't even know you could count that high . . . ," Eli muttered under his breath.

Steve flexed his biceps, inadvertently stepping in between Eli and their favorite TV star. But even with his blocked view, Eli saw just how much the other two had in common. Steve could have been a younger version of the actor. Both were tall, blond, muscular—pretty much the exact opposite of Eli, who felt more like a fifth wheel than ever. He pulled the top half of the Octopoid outfit over his pouting face and slumped toward the exit . . . just as Foo-Foo's drone descended into the lounge.

Its sensors scanned every living being in the VIP area, as they had done in the lost-and-found booth and long bathroom lines before that. Not detecting anything out of the ordinary, the drone was about to hover away—until it spied Eli in the Octopoid suit. Its camera zoomed in on the tentacle-covered shape, and a new entry of data scrolled across its view screen.

Extraterrestrial life-form: detected

Classification: cephaloplasmus. Zorkian

Additional information: wanted in several solar systems/open bounty of eight million crestons for immediate capture/LETHAL FORCE PERMITTED

Primary directive: Per Foo-Foo the Destroyer. survey area from above/neutralize any encountered extraterrestrials/NEUTRALIZE—NEUTRALIZE—NEUTRALIZE

Crosshairs appeared on its screen. Two miniature blasters swiveled into place. And without any warning, the drone opened fire on an unsuspecting Elijah Leslie Pepperjack.

CHAPTER 12
WANTED DEAD OR ALIVELY

"I have the news that is bad and the news that is less bad," Krel said to Aja. "Which would you like to receive first?"

The siblings had just found each other in the food court, where Aja drank directly from the nacho cheese dispenser, trying to fill her stomach—if not the emptiness she felt in her core. A vague sense of failure had followed Aja from the fashion exhibit. The more she thought about those warrior queens on display, the more she felt she didn't match their level of posterior-kicking-ness. Wiping the molten cheese off her face, Aja said, "The news that is bad, I suppose."

"I have located Varvatos Vex at a human gaming tournament," answered Krel.

"How is that bad?" asked Aja.

"Because he's acting just like Varvatos Vex at a human gaming tournament!" said Krel.

"BELAYA!" they heard Vex shout again from afar. "Destiny has rolled a hard six and comes to deplete you of your health points! So swears Varvatos Vex of the Taylon Phalanx—and now the Guild of the Wizard Knights! Huzzah!"

"Huzzah!" echoed a nasal, nerdy chorus.

"And the less-bad news?" Aja asked.

Krel pointed at the fine print on his Arcadia-Con badge and said, "These passes admit us into the *Gun Robot* premiere. We do not even have to sleep in that shantytown outside!"

"I see," Aja said glumly. "And you want us to go into the theater and make fun of the movie."

"Er, I suppose," Krel said. "Although I am now more interested in the movie's story than in its faulty logic. This Gun Robot fellow *intrigues* me. . . ."

Krel surprised himself, even as he said the words. True, he had gone into Arcadia-Con expecting the very worst humanity had to offer. And in many cases, he'd seen it.

Then again, in thinking back to his undisputed

reign at the *Go-Go Sushi* dance floor, Krel discovered that his stance had softened. *Somewhat.* For once, people on this planet complimented him instead of questioned him. Krel had identified several of them from school earlier—and identified *with* them. No matter their age, gender, or ethnicity, it seemed to the displaced princeling that these teens all had one thing in common: They felt uncomfortable in their own skins. Just like Krel did on Earth.

"No, thank you, little brother," said Aja. "I am not feeling up it right this mekron."

"Is it the mass quantities of processed-cheese product you consumed?" asked Krel.

"No—*urp!*" Aja belched. "Although that probably isn't helping."

She took a few steps forward, her high-top sneakers sticking to the syrupy, soda-coated floors. Thousands of people enjoyed themselves all around Aja, their grinning faces beaming at the various diversions that competed for their attention. Mother had landed in Arcadia Oaks not long ago, yet Aja was hard-pressed to recall a time when she saw so many humans so happy.

"It's all just so . . . overwhelming," Aja said to Krel. "Why is it that so many of these humans appear more cheerful in their pretend costumes than in their normal lives? All the characters they seek to emulate are just that: characters. Fiction. Figments of imagination that they will never match, no matter how hard they might try. Are humans so disappointed, so *lost*, that they must turn to make-believe stories to find solace—to truly feel alive?"

"Well, when you put it *that* way . . . ," Krel said, trying to reconcile Aja's feelings about Arcadia-Con with his own. "Perhaps it is for the best that the humans are distracted by their silly legends. Perhaps that makes it easier for us to complete our Daxial Array and return to . . ."

Krel trailed off when an ominous shadow fell over them. Foo-Foo stood atop a nearby food court table and said in his flat, affectless voice, "Aja and Krel Tarron, by order of General Val Morando, you are wanted war criminals. I am Foo-Foo the Destroyer and I'll destroy—"

"Ooh, bunny!" Aja cooed as she ran over and picked up Foo-Foo.

The bounty hunter wriggled and squirmed while

Aja buried her face in his belly. She came up for air and said in a baby talk, "Who's a lively little bunny? You are! Yes, you!"

"I must cuddle him," Krel said as he scratched behind Foo-Foo's ear.

"Put me down!" Foo-Foo protested, trying to maintain some dignity as they petted him.

He broke free of their affectionate grasps, unsheathed the hard-light dagger, and said, "At first, I was apprehensive about hunting you across this enclosed, populated space. But the local life-forms here are so desensitized to sights beyond their understanding, they will do nothing to come between me and my bounty!"

Foo-Foo waved his dagger at the masses milling around them. Only a few attendees paid him any notice before looking back at their phones. Aja and Krel both realized that Foo-Foo was right— and that they were still without their Serrators.

The hard-light blade sang as it sliced through the stale food court air. The royals barely dodged the strike, then looked at each other, desperate for a way to defend themselves. Krel started moving his feet like he was back on the *Go-Go Sushi* dance floor, flossing his arms in front and behind his hips. The movement distracted Foo-Foo long enough for Aja to reach the nacho station and shout, "Hey, Foo-Foo! Say 'cheese'!"

The queen-in-waiting bent the spout upward and squirted out an entire gallon of molten cheese. The yellow goo streamed over Krel's shoulder and splatted onto Foo-Foo. His armor hit the floor with a resounding clang. Only a few convention goers bothered to look up from their fast food and comics. Foo-Foo tried to stand again, but his cybernetic feet slipped on the viscous puddle. He shook his fist at the royals and roared, "You Akiridion adolescents will pay for this affront—with your cores!"

"Awwwww!" Aja and Krel said adoringly.

"So cute," added Aja.

"So helpless," added Krel.

"Foo-Foo the Destroyer is not cute!" said Foo-Foo. "And I am far from helpless!"

He popped a hatch on his back and ejected two more of the traps he used to ensnare his Gumm-Gumms. Aja and Krel took off down the nearest aisle, zigzagging between preoccupied attendees. But the traps rocketed after them, matching the siblings turn for turn as if they were heat-seeking missiles. The royals had just reached the next section of Arcadia-Con, when shackles clamped down onto their ankles. They tripped and fell into some folding tables and chairs.

Foo-Foo's suit made its telltale springing sound as he hopped over and watched Aja and Krel writhe on the floor. Although his metal face remained impassive, the bounty hunter still had the air of someone who gloated. He pressed another button on his wrist guard, and the two traps responded. The devices each projected a series of intersecting beams, sealing Aja and Krel in a single glowing cage of pure energy. A few Arcadia-Con attendees took notice of this new light show, and Foo-Foo tapped another button. The cage's bars started to constrict around the royals.

"We still think you're adorable!" Aja said as she pushed in vain against the bars.

"I don't care," replied the rabbitlike creature. "House Tarron once interfered with my destiny, and I won't let it happen again. Once you two are out of the way, none shall stand between Varvatos and me ever again!"

CHAPTER 13
INTERCEPTED COMMUNICATIONS

"Frightened yet?" whispered Zadra.

Davaros thought over the question as they hid behind a wall in the royal palace of Akiridion. The girl then nodded and asked, "Are you disappointed in me?"

Now it was Zadra's turn to think. When she had been a lowly cadet, the Taylon Phalanx trained its recruits to never be afraid—that fear was a sign of weakness. But as Zadra rose through their ranks, she came to understand that the opposite was true. Whether she ran an obstacle course or battled an enemy combatant to the death, Zadra's fear kept her nerves on edge. Those nerves kept her senses sharp. Those senses kept her aware. And that awareness kept Zadra alive long enough to become lieutenant.

"Not at all," Zadra told Davaros.

Zadra waited for the surveillance orb to move past on its preprogrammed route, then signaled for Davaros to follow her. They left the wall, paused behind a pillar to avoid another orb, then reached the ascensor. Zadra punched in an access code, while Davaros made sure they remained undetected. A door slid open, and they stepped onto a disc, which lifted them upward.

Zadra winked at Davaros to bolster the young girl's confidence. But Davaros kept quiet. Rather than force a conversation, which was never Zadra's strong suit anyway, she decided to let Davaros remain silent. Because that meant the girl was afraid. And that fear meant she just might survive.

The ascensor reached the top floor of the citadel. Zadra and Davaros exited onto a floor populated entirely by Blank units. The closest Blank turned its sleek white head and said, "Greetings, Lieutenant Zadra. How may we assist you in the communications sector today?"

Davaros watched Zadra's six nimble fingers rewire the Blank's innards, just as Izita had taught her. A moment later the eyes on the Blank unit went from distressed red squiggles to mellow green dots. This effect then spread to the other robots on the floor. The Blanks returned to their work terminals. Each keystroke they made on the holographic displays set off a symphony of melodic chimes.

"Their memory banks will now auto-wipe every three sectons," said Zadra. "To them it will seem as if we were never here."

She and Davaros sidestepped the hot-wired Blanks and entered another room. The door hissed shut behind them, sealing the pair inside a technology bay. Soft, pink light bathed a sophisticated array of computer processors. Behind the machines a wall of floor-to-ceiling windows offered a dizzying view of Akiridion far below. Davaros pointed to the central server and said, "That's what we'll need to trace the Pingpod. I just never realized it'd be so big!"

"Nor did I," said Zadra before suddenly going very, very still. "Do you hear that?"

Davaros strained to listen, but heard nothing other than the gentle whir of the servers. She gave the lieutenant a quizzical look and said, "No?"

"Exactly," said Zadra, pulling the scythe from her back and flicking out its blades. "The computers outside aren't chiming. The Blanks have stopped working. We're not alone."

The lighting in the technology bay turned from pink to crimson. Zadra grabbed Davaros's wrist with her free hand and pulled her closer. A half second later the door glided open once more, revealing a regiment of loyalist soldiers. They fixed their one-eyed helmets on the two rebel intruders. The loyalists then parted down the middle, making way for their leader—General Val Morando.

"Why, Lieutenant, what brings you to this sector?" asked Morando, his gossamer cape billowing as he circled. "I didn't think communications was one of your *specialities* . . ."

Zadra's mind raced. She tried to envision a way to take out Morando and his guards long enough for Davaros to escape. But every imagined scenario ended only in capture—or worse.

"Curse you, Zadra!" Davaros shouted abruptly, surprising everyone, Zadra included. Zadra stared at Davaros in shock.

Davaros twisted her arm around in Zadra's hand so that it looked like she was the lieutenant's captive, not compatriot. Morando's four eyes became suspicious slits. Davaros said, "I'm not afraid of you, Morando! I and my fellow rebels still recognize House Tarron as the one, true authority of Akiridion! Your lieutenant may have apprehended me before I could complete my mission, but fear not! Two more Resistance spies will surely rise to take my place!"

For a long moment all anyone heard was the faint hum of the servers. Zadra blinked at Davaros, impressed by her skill for improvisation, but deeply worried for what would come next. In assuming all the blame, Davaros had endangered herself. Yet she had also protected Zadra's identity as a double agent, a mole embedded at the highest level of Morando's forces.

"Is this true, Lieutenant Zadra?" the general finally asked.

Zadra took one last look into Davaros's eyes, which so closely resembled her mother's. She tried to imagine what Izita would choose in this moment—the fate of the entire Resistance or the life of her own child. In a voice just above a whisper, Zadra said, "It . . . it's true. All of it."

Davaros nodded almost imperceptibly at her,

like she was proud of the woman assigned to protect her. If this girl felt any more fear at the moment, Zadra could not see it. Morando tipped his head toward them and said, "Take the child to Sector Black for elimination."

Zadra shut her eyes in resignation. She felt Morando's guards wrench Davaros out of her hand. To the girl's credit she never cried or begged. She only looked back with a deadpan expression on her way out. Morando bared his fangs into a smile and said, "Well done, Lieutenant. To be sure, I had been worried about infiltration in my inner circle. How fortunate for me, then, that you are here to keep your general safe."

His gaze lingered on her for a moment longer. Then Morando turned on his heels and strode out of the communications area. Zadra watched him go, followed by the loyalists escorting Davaros. More flashbacks from Zadra's many tours of duty flooded her core. To Zadra, watching Davaros be sent to Sector Black felt like losing another fellow soldier. She felt utterly helpless and miserable but refused to let it show. To Zadra, it felt like Xerexes's Maelstrom all over again.

CHAPTER 14
THE AMAZING CHASE

"Wait! I want to see what happens next!" whined Mary. "Can't we stay? Please?"

Team Trollhunters hustled her, Darci, and Shannon deeper into the *Murder House* maze, with Foo-Foo's Gumm-Gumms in hot pursuit. The three girls had watched Jim tell his very tall friend in the monster getup to make a path. So the big guy rammed his mossy shoulder into a wall and punched a giant hole right through the labyrinth. Mary, Darci, and Shannon had giggled as the others then pushed them through the impromptu escape route. But now they felt like they were being rushed past the attraction's best parts.

"Quit shoving, Toby-Pie!" Darci said.

Toby yelped and tackled his girlfriend. A

split-second later, a Parlok spear flew through the spot where Darci's head had been. The weapon splintered the painted plywood above them.

"Solid scare!" said Shannon, admiring what she assumed was a special effect.

Jim and Claire hurriedly ushered along Shannon and the others. The three wire-infested Gumm-Gumms still pursued them relentlessly. Pouring on the speed, Jim considered the Amulet in his hand and said, "We've gotta stop running and start defending ourselves!"

"Yeah, but ditching Mary, Darci, and Shannon won't be easy!" Claire said between coughs. "As far as they—*koff!*—know, they're having the time of their—*koff!*—lives!"

"Aw, for the luvva Glug!" groused NotEnrique, who had been hanging on to Claire's back the entire time. "Do I gotta do everythin' 'round here?"

He hopped off Claire and scampered ahead. Because of his small stature and sneaky nature, NotEnrique easily scooted past Mary, Darci, and Shannon without being seen. He took turn after turn, eventually reaching a dead end. NotEnrique's pug face curled into a smile, and he said, "Perfect . . ."

A few yards back, Mary, Darci, and Shannon moved to the head of the pack and followed the same series of twists and turns in the maze. They chattered excitedly, eagerly anticipating the next jump scare the *Murder House* had to offer. Reaching a blind alley, the girls playfully argued over who should go in first. Mary then "volunteered" Shannon by pushing her forward.

Shannon stumbled, accidentally tripping into the dead end. Her glasses fell off, and she groped blindly on floor, which was carpeted in fog. With blurry vision, Shannon thought she saw a dark shape slumped in the corner—a dark shape that *moved*.

"H-hello?" Shannon called out, still fumbling for her glasses. "Do you work here?"

"Shan? You okay in there?" called Darci as she and Mary joined her.

"Who were you talking to?" Mary asked, finding the glasses and giving them to Shannon.

Shannon put them on, and now able to see again, she said, "There was someone down there."

The girls looked at the dead end. It was empty. Shannon startled when she spotted that same dark shape now slumped a few feet closer. Mary saw that it was wearing a diaper. She rolled her eyes and said, "Ugh, it's just some rubber baby doll. Yawn."

Although NotEnrique had recently lost the ability to change his shape, he still retained the size and proportions of a human infant—albeit a furry, green one. But those Trollish features remained obscured by the maze's smoke machines and dim lighting. Just as Mary, Darci, and Shannon were about to leave, NotEnrique turned his little head toward them.

The girls caught the movement in their peripheral vision and screamed, "AAAAAAAH!"

NotEnrique stood up, his Changeling eyes shining yellow in the darkness.

Again they screamed.

The wee Changeling toddler-walked down the corridor toward them, the flashing strobe lights making his gait appear all the more stilted and unnatural.

Yet more screams.

NotEnrique then held out his chubby little arms and, in his most childlike voice, said, "Baby hungry—for *blood*!"

The girls' final screams were so loud and so long, Mary fainted from a lack of oxygen. Shannon and Darci caught her and ran shrieking back the way they came. NotEnrique dusted his hands in satisfaction and said, "Gets 'em every time!"

Team Trollhunters jumped as Darci and Shannon rushed by in the opposite direction, dragging the unconscious Mary along with them. Shannon wailed in hysterics and said to Claire, "Don't go that way, C-Bomb! It's horrible! *Horrible!*"

"Um, bye-bye, boo?" Toby said with a weak wave to Darci.

The girls bolted past the three Gumm-Gumms, who seemed equally surprised. With this portion of the maze now cleared of innocent bystanders and witnesses, both sides prepared for battle. The Amulet shone in Jim's hand, and he incanted, "For the doom of Gunmar, Eclipse is mine to command!"

A geyser of black-and-red magic spiraled out of the device and around Jim. The Gumm-Gumms shielded their eyes from the supernatural spectacle, then saw the Trollhunter standing before them in his obsidian Eclipse Armor. Jim's teammates quickly followed suit. Blinky raised four fists, AAARRRGGHH!!! cracked his knuckles, and Claire extended her Shadow Staff.

"Decided to go for a darker look this time, huh, Jimbo?" Toby asked of the Eclipse Armor.

Jim retracted the faceplate from his horned helmet and said, "Guess I was inspired by the *Murder House* décor, Tobes."

"Then let's stay on-brand and hold a demo day for these Gumm-Gumms!" said Toby.

His Warhammer connected with one of the evil Troll's skulls. Jim manifested the Sword of Eclipse in his hand and drove the ebon blade through the dazed brute, turning him to solid stone. Blinky grabbed another Gumm-Gumm with one pair of his hands—then used the other pair to shove Dwärkstone grenades under his armor. Claire opened a shadow portal as the Gumm-Gumm frantically tried dislodging the bombs. AAARRRGGHH!!! then rammed into him, sending him spinning into the infinite vacuum of the Shadow Realm.

"In space, no one can hear you explode!" said Blinky.

The black portal cinched itself shut just as the

grenades detonated, muting most of the resultant blast. And the final Gumm-Gumm, now outnumbered five to one, fled. The Trollhunter detached the Glaives from his thighs, connected the interlocking blades, and hurled the single curved weapon. It struck the retreating Gumm-Gumm in his circuit-riddled back, reducing him to another lifeless statue. Now petrified, the Troll teetered over and shattered.

"Out of all our victories, this has to be the most a-*maze*-ing, right, guys?" Toby said with a wag of his eyebrows.

Blinky slapped four hands against his forehead and moaned, "Master Jim was mistaken. The frights we faced here were nothing compared to Tobias's terrible puns."

"Hashtag lame," grumbled AAARRRGGHH!!!

Jim knelt to retrieve his Glaives from the broken Gumm-Gumm on the floor, then noticed the foreign circuitry still mixed in with the rest of the rubble. The Trollhunter tugged on the wires and followed them till they eventually led him to one of Foo-Foo's neural control discs.

"What in the world do you suppose this is?" Jim

asked. "If it even *is* from this world . . ."

The disc and wires spontaneously combusted in his hands, as did the filaments on the other felled Gumm-Gumm. The maze's overhead lights turned on then, washing Team Trollhunters in a harsh fluorescent glare. As their eyes adjusted, they realized how shoddy the labyrinth looked when it wasn't lit just right. Jim and the others then heard a stampede of footsteps coming from one direction and the squawk of walkie-talkies from the other.

"It sounds like somebody noticed our recent renovations," Toby guessed. "Whoops."

Jim said, "Claire, I hate to ask this, but are you well enough to shadow-jump us home?"

"M-maybe not that far," she answered unsteadily. "But I might be able to send us someplace a little closer."

Team Trollhunters ducked into the new swirling shadow Claire summoned. NotEnrique ran over on all fours and said, "Don't forget yer backpack!"

The Changeling disappeared into the portal with the others, just before it winked out of existence—and just before several Arcadia-Con security guards filed into the maze. They stared at all the destruction done to the official *Murder House* fan experience and at the strange gravel crunching under their feet. One of the shocked guards unclipped his walkie-talkie and said, "Uh, come in, central. You're never gonna believe what we just found. . . ."

"Copy that," said the voice on the other end. "We're getting strange reports coming in from all over the Con. Requesting immediate assistance at the main entrance—over!"

CHAPTER 15
SLAYING WITH SWAGGER

A laser shot straight through the top of Octopoid costume, grazing the cowlick on Eli's head. He wrinkled his nose at the unexpected smell of burning hair, then noticed the smoking holes leading into and out of his cosplay costume. Standing on the tips of his toes, Eli looked out of the entry wound and saw a drone hovering a few feet away. Everyone else in the VIP lounge—including Steve and his acting idol—was too busy hobnobbing to notice the flying robot. The drone detected Eli's eye peering out of the tentacled husk and began recalculating.

Extraterrestrial life-form: Classification error/not cephaloplasmus. Zorkian

Primary directive: Per Foo-Foo the Destroyer, leave no witnesses

Secondary directive: TERMINATE—TERMINATE—TERMINATE

Eli screamed as the drone's miniblasters unleashed a fresh fusillade of lasers. They perforated the Octopoid outfit, making Swiss cheese of the latex. The shredded top half of the suit tipped over, revealing nothing but empty space beneath it. As the drone processed this, a pair of zip slippers poked out from under a table loaded with *Earth Invaders* promotional items—posters, oversize novelty bags, T-shirts, and more. Eli had slipped out of the costume once the drone lit it up. But when Eli saw the drone's shadow cross in front of the table, the Creepslayer realized he was cornered.

Eli scrolled through the emergency contacts on his cell. His trembling finger hesitated over the first name—Steve. But in remembering their recent spat, Eli just couldn't bring himself to ask for Steve's help. He was about to call Jim, when the drone descended to Eli's eye level.

"Ah!" Eli screamed.

The drone locked its crosshairs on Eli's frightened face—and a silver tray slammed into it like it were a discus. Knocked off balance, the drone wobbled to the far end of the lounge. Eli ran out from under the table and saw Steve holding a tray full of canapes. The brawny Creepslayer yelled, "Buzz off, bot-snack!"

"Steve!" Eli cried with joy, then remembered he was still mad. "You, uh, didn't have to do that. I can take care of myself!"

"Oh yeah? How?" Steve asked. "By hiding under another swag table?"

"Maybe!" Eli hollered. "Or maybe I'll use my other self-defense skills! Skills you've never even bothered to learn about!"

"Such drama!" said the actor who played Superagent Muldoon.

The *Earth Invaders* star and the rest of the Hollywood elite had been watching Steve and Eli's argument. The actor then said, "Fans often post short videos on my social media feed. But I've never seen a live scene before! I'm really believing the *pain* in your performance."

The drone veered at them again, and Eli said,

"Quick! Creepslayer combo fifty-two!"

"On it!" said Steve.

He picked up Eli by the seat of his pants and tossed him at the drone. The airborne robot avoided the screaming Eli, who bounced off the wall. He shot Steve a dirty look from behind his crooked glasses and said, "That was combo twenty-five!"

"Oh," said Steve as the drone aimed its cannons at him. "Right."

"Combo eight-six-niner!" Eli shouted.

Steve leaped forward and was about to use his teammate's back as a springboard to launch himself high. But Eli abruptly turned around and crowed, "Ca-caw!"

The Creepslayerz collided, knocking over the swag table. They peeled *Earth Invaders* bumper stickers off their faces, and Eli shouted, "I said 'eight-six-niner'—distract and divide! The bent-back spring attack is a nine-six-eight!"

"*You're* a nine-six-eight!" Steve shouted back.

Superagent Muldoon and the rest of the Very Important People laughed, assuming this skit had now become a comedy of errors. Steve's scowl only intensified as he experienced the feeling he hated above all others—humiliation. The drone wheeled around again, and Steve shoved Eli aside, saying, "Forget the combos! This time, the Palchuk goes solo!"

Steve ducked and rolled away from another volley of lasers, while Eli stumbled backward and fell on his rear. Experiencing his own flush of humiliation, Eli muttered, "Fine, Steve. If you want to take all the glory—and the death beams—you go right ahead. . . ."

Superagent Muldoon crouched beside Eli and said, "As a fellow method actor, I respect your process. And I'd never want to break the fourth wall. But I must say that I question your motivation in the moment."

"Huh?" said Eli.

Talking over Steve's terrified shrieks in the background, the star said, "You're assuming your friend is pushing you away to be mean. But what if he's pushing you away to *protect* you?"

Eli looked back at Steve. His teammate alternately taunted and cried as he wrestled with the drone. Realization dawned in Eli's eyes, and the actor added, "Y'know, I was a lot like you growing up. Envious of the bigger guys who got all the attention. But if my career's taught me anything, it's that the little guy can *also* make a difference. Sure, I may play the 'big hero' on TV, but Superagent Muldoon is only as good as the material the show's screenwriters give him. In theater and in life, it's all about collaboration."

"Collaboration," Eli repeated slowly. "You're right. Steve needs me!"

With a click of his heels, he activated his zip slippers and skated toward his teammate. Along the way, Eli took a slight detour at the swag table. Steve grunted as the drone pinned him to the lounge floor, the two of them struggling for control of the laser blasters. The barrels gradually pointed closer to Steve's face, no matter how hard he pushed against them. The chambers started glowing, ready to fire—when an enormous sack scooped up the drone. Steve saw Eli restraining the drone inside one of the oversized *Earth Invaders* novelty bags.

"Eli?" Steve said in amazement. "You saved me? Even after I botched our combos?"

"Just like you saved me, even after I lost my temper with you," replied Eli. "I think I got so caught up in us being Creepslayerz, I forgot we also need to be collaboratorz."

The drone launched skyward, taking the giant bag—and Eli—with it. His skinny legs kicking helplessly in the air, Eli said, "Steve! The table!"

"On it!" Steve said again.

Only this time Steve actually understood what he was doing. He raced over to the swag table and picked up something he saw earlier, when he and Eli had crashed into it. With a devious grin, Steve cocked the T-shirt cannon in his hands and said, "You call out the plans, Pepperbuddy—and I *execute* them!"

"Engage!" Eli shouted from the ceiling.

Steve aimed and pulled the trigger, shooting out a rolled-up *Earth Invaders* T-shirt with a tremendous *FWOOMP!* The preshrunk projectile whizzed through the air and struck the drone with a direct hit.

"Spectacular!" cried Eli before he and the drone plummeted. "Ah!"

"Uh, couch cushion combo!" said Steve.

Thinking fast, he slid one of the lounge sofas into place. Eli landed safely on the plush furniture, while the drone smashed into pieces on the floor beside him. Steve and Eli exchanged relieved smiles, and the VIP guests broke into enthusiastic applause. Superagent Muldoon said, "Bravo, guys! And way to take those emotional adjustments on the fly!"

"It helps when you have a great 'scene partner'!" Eli said with a wink to Steve.

Steve winked back and said, "You're way too talented to be my 'understudy,' Eli. I promise, the next time the Creepslayerz go into action, they're gonna have equal billing."

Eli's grin grew bigger, and the *Earth Invaders* star said, "I know you guys probably don't want to leave the VIP area, but I'd love for you to be my guests at the *Gun Robot* premiere. I play a crusty FBI agent who can only reunite with his estranged daughter through Gun Robot's help. Powerful stuff. So . . . whattaya say?"

The Creepslayerz looked at each other in wonderment and flashed their C hand symbol.

"I've got a *bad* feeling about this," said Detective Louis Scott.

The Arcadia Oaks police department banged

a battering ram against the Convention Center's shuttered main entrance with zero effect. Officer Brennan came running up and said, "It's the same thing at the rear gate, loading dock, and emergency exits. We can't get in, and the Arcadia-Con attendees can't get out! This is a dangerous situation."

"Including my daughter," said Detective Scott as he thought about his Darci.

The insistent banging of the battering ram resonated inside of the Convention Center, making Luug hold his paws over his ears. He didn't know what exactly was going on, but he suspected it had something to do with that tasty-looking bunnylike creature. With all the guards otherwise occupied, Luug raised his leg and zapped a hole in the kennel's fence. Several spooked canines backed away in alarm as the Corgi jumped through the hole and made a beeline for the security desk. Luug sniffed until he found what he was looking for—Aja's and Krel's Serrators.

CHAPTER 16
ROLL REVERSAL

"If it is any consolation, I know how you must feel," Foo-Foo said as Aja and Krel struggled in the shrinking cage. "Caught. Alone against impossible odds. Left for dead on a foreign world. Any last words?"

"BELAYA!"

Foo-Foo looked up just in time to see a debonair human crash into him. Both the bounty hunter and the actor who portrayed Detective Jim Belaya groaned in pain. The cage stopped closing in on Aja and Krel, its movement halted by the impact on Foo-Foo's wrist guard.

Vex hobbled across the gaming pavilion with his cane, knelt in front of the trapped teens, and said, "Remain calm, Royals. You shall be freed in a mekron. If only Nana Domzalski could have witnessed how easily Belaya was bested in the death duel . . . instead of searching for her indolent soolian of a grandson."

Foo-Foo didn't recognize the human's wrinkled face, but he could never forget his voice—nor the wild gleam in his eyes, even though Vex only had two now instead four.

"Varvatos! Varvatos! It's me! Foo-Foo the Destroyer!" Foo-Foo said beneath Belaya. "Remember? We met at Xerexes's Maelstrom? Well, *almost* met . . ."

Vex tried to pull the cage's light bars apart with his bare hands, grunting, "The commander of the Taylon Phalanx has met many beings on the battlefield, both friend and foe. Yet Varvatos does not recall ever making your acquaintance. Surely Varvatos would remember encountering one with such comically large ears."

"You . . . don't remember?" Foo-Foo asked as pulled his last foot free from under Belaya. "Well, let's fix that! We should hang out sometime and—"

"Varvatos Vex does not 'hang out,'" said Vex, giving up on the impenetrable bars.

"But . . . but . . . but I've followed you—stalked

you—across the entire universe," Foo-Foo said, his voice modulator making him sound all the more inhuman. "Aren't you proud?"

"'Proud'?" Vex spat, finally regarding Foo-Foo. "Proud that you've endangered the cores of two children? No, Varvatos Vex could *never* be proud of any who would engage in so ignoble a profession as bounty hunting."

Foo-Foo looked away in shame and said, "I . . . I was in a bad place after Xerexes. I sort of fell into the whole bounty hunting thing. Besides, who cares about these royals? They don't get you like *I* do. Once they're out of the way, you and I can—"

"There is no 'you and I,' Foo-Foo," Vex interrupted. "Nor will there ever be. Varvatos Vex has room in his life for only two clueless, needy creatures—and those creatures are Aja and Krel Tarron!"

"Thank you, Varvatos!" Aja said sincerely.

"Your words honor us!" Krel added just as earnestly.

"No," Foo-Foo said flatly. "You are just confused, Varvatos. Your time with these juveniles on this planet has clouded your vision. It won't let you see the truth."

"The only truth Varvatos sees is how a sad, little critter has obsessed about some chance encounter for far too long," said Vex.

Foo-Foo stopped talking. The servos on his mechanical eyes shifted as he saw his idol in a different light. Without warning or emotion Foo-Foo tapped the controls on his arm, compacting the cage once more.

"I will make you see me the way I see you, Varvatos," vowed Foo-Foo. "Even if I must kill them to do it!"

"Wait!" Vex shouted, pounding his cane on the ground for emphasis. "Your quarrel is not with the Tarron royals. Or with any of the innocent—yet deeply misguided—who-mans who have crammed their flabby and overexposed bodies into this endless bunker."

A few of the Arcadia-Con attendees who had been eavesdropping lowered their heads and sucked in their guts. Aja and Krel looked from them back to Vex, their faces pressed tight against the quantum bars of the narrowing cage.

"No, your grudge lies solely with Varvatos Vex, though Varvatos knows not why," said Vex. "But what if there was some other way to make Varvatos *proud* of you?"

"What . . . what is it you propose?" asked Foo-Foo, unable to hide his interest.

"A test of strategy and mental acumen," said Vex. "The *ultimate* match of wits—a who-man deck-building card game."

Foo-Foo's ears twitched as he weighed the offer. More of the surrounding convention guests perked up and shuffled closer. Feeling all their eyes on him, the bounty hunter said, "This is some sort of trick. A lie."

"Varvatos Vex is not given to perfidy and has only lied once in his long life," said Vex, averting his eyes as he recalled his betrayal of Aja and Krel's parents.

Of course, the two young royals could not have known what their bodyguard thought in the moment. They were currently preoccupied with getting out of their cage—and with the darling little bounty hunter who had trapped them within it.

"I can't stand it!" Aja whispered. "Even when he's angry, he's so klebbing cute!"

"Rest assured, Varvatos Vex holds no advantage

over you, as Varvatos only barely comprehends this needlessly complicated game," said Vex.

"Hmm . . . and the stakes?" asked Foo-Foo, mulling it over.

"If Varvatos wins, you will release the royals, leave Earth, and forfeit your bounty," Vex said. "However, if Varvatos *loses*, then Varvatos will hand you Aja's and Krel's cores himself."

"Vex!" said Aja.

"No!" cried Krel.

Vex studied Foo-Foo, who actually seemed to consider the terms. The bounty hunter appeared close to accepting the deal. So Vex decided to sweeten it, adding, "You did want to 'hang out' with Varvatos Vex, did you not?"

"More than anything," answered Foo-Foo.

"Then put your crestons where your chew-hole is and let the Maze Master deal you in!" finished Vex.

A pudgy teen in a wizard's robe genuflected with a flourish before Foo-Foo, shuffling cards as he bowed. The bounty hunter looked from Vex to the caged Aja and Krel, then back to Vex. After a tense beat, he said, "Very well. Foo-Foo the Destroyer accepts your challenge."

Foo-Foo paused the cage's movements, and the relieved Aja and Krel sighed as much as their cramped bodies would let them. Vex then motioned to one of the few folding tables they hadn't knocked over. He and Foo-Foo sat at opposite ends, never taking their eyes off each other. The Maze Master dealt out cards, puffed on his asthma inhaler, and said, "Mark my words, ye who are about to venture into the realm of Mazes and Monsters. On this, the first eve of Arcadia-Con, a senior citizen and, um, robo-rabbit have entered freely and of their own wills into . . . a sudden death campaign!"

A hushed murmur spread across the growing crowd as the duly appointed Maze Master explained the rest of the rules. Inside the quantum cage Aja and Krel looked at each other with apprehension, their noses and lips smooshed against the bars. The Maze Master held up a quieting hand, and order was restored to the gaming pavilion. He then handed the thirteen-sided die to Foo-Foo and said, "As ever, the challenged has first roll. Let the game . . . BEGIN!"

The pubescent Maze Master's voice cracked on that last word, yet no one noticed. They were far too enrapt in the tournament. Foo-Foo rolled a five, flipped over his first card, and said, "Aha! A Mirror Mage! Deduct five health points, Varv. May I call you 'Varv'?"

Vex grunted as if he had been injured in real life, then turned his health card sideways and slid it halfway into his deck. He took the die next, blew on it for luck as Nana had shown him, and rolled an eleven.

"Glorious!" boomed Vex, turning over his Orc Spy and Immortal Chalice cards. "Varvatos Vex casts a rejuvenation spell and strikes at you with the fabled Fireblade!"

Foo-Foo slammed a fist on the table, cursing in his native tongue. And so it went, back and forth, point and counterpoint, for the better part of an hour. Aja cheered as Vex stole Foo-Foo's Queen of Curiosities card. Krel's teeth gritted when Foo-Foo rolled a wild two, skipping Vex's next turn and doing double damage. And the attendees of Arcadia-Con— be they young or old, costumed or not—held their collective breaths as the Maze Master announced the final roll. Foo-Foo swirled the die in his paw, tossed it across the game board, and saw the thirteen come up. He thrust his armored arms into the air and shouted, "Yes! That thirteen—coupled with my Horn of Uriel and Iron King cards—makes a critical roll! I win!"

Half the crowd cheered for Foo-Foo, while the other half groaned in disappointment. Aja and Krel looked at Vex, who appeared resigned to defeat. He tossed his remaining cards onto the table and said, "It would appear that chance favors the bold." He held his remaining three cards tightly. Foo-Foo leveled his eyes at the Tarron children. He prepared to power up their cage once more and squeeze them into nothingness. Aja and Krel held hands, fearing the worst.

"And yet," Vex added loudly, "preparation favors the cunning. For Varvatos Vex has been holding a Roll Reversal card this entire time!"

He turned over his middle card, and the assorted gamers around him gasped in surprise. Vex stood up mightily, held his cane aloft like a knight's sword, and yelled, "Varvatos Vex is glorious—*and* victorious!"

Foo-Foo the Destroyer stared in disbelief at the card, even as Aja, Krel, and the rest of the tournament spectators cheered for Vex. Honoring their agreement, the bounty hunter deactivated the quantum cage, releasing the royals. Now able to breathe fully again, Aja and Krel hugged.

"You played well," said Vex. "Perhaps Foo-Foo the Destroyer and Commander Varvatos Vex could have been friends, had things gone differently on Xerexes."

Vex's sentiments caused something to snap deep inside Foo-Foo's impenetrable shell. He forgot all about making Commander Vex proud or the outcome of their recent wager. With lightning-fast speed, Foo-Foo the Destroyer lunged at the royals.

Time seemed to slow down for Aja as the lunatic rabbit creature leaped at her and her brother. She glanced to the side, seeing stunned attendees dressed as dragon princesses, Viking Valkyries, and postapocalyptic female freedom fighters. And in the span of a second, Aja Tarron knew what she should do—what a warrior queen must always do. Aja positioned herself directly in front of Krel and let Foo-Foo's hard-light dagger stab her in chest.

No commander ever wishes to lose a soldier. But hard choices must be made in war.

Varvatos Vex's words still haunted Zadra. She had always looked up to her commander. Vex was the one who trained Zadra in combat. Who fought alongside Zadra at Xerexes's Maelstrom. Who assigned Zadra to her most cherished post— safeguarding Aja and Krel.

But Vex was also the one who conspired with Morando. Were Coranda and Fialkov just two more hard choices made by Vex in a time of war? Zadra once took her commander's lesson as an immutable law that had to be obeyed. But now, it seemed like so much—

"Klebso," Zadra said out loud.

She appraised the communications rig in the palace's technology bay. Its outer casing was far too big to fit under Zadra's sleeves. But a new plan of attack formed in Zadra's mind . . .

"What are you planning?" shouted a loyalist through his featureless faceplate. "What does the Resistance want with our comms systems? What do they know about OMEN?"

Davaros refused to answer, even as another loyalist shoved her into a cylindrical chamber deep within Sector Black—a small room lined with onyx panels and various implements of torture. A third soldier tapped commands into a console, the red eye on his helmet never blinking. The chamber door closed, sealing Davaros into a transparent coffin.

"Core extractor optimized and ready," said the loyalist at the controls.

The door to Sector Black opened behind the trio of loyalists. Their cyclopean helmets swiveled and saw a fourth loyalist, his tactical armor matching their own riot gear.

"New orders from Morando," the fourth figure said. "Stand down."

"What?" asked the loyalist at the controls. "I don't see any order on my terminal to belay."

"Is that so?" asked the late arrival, who held a staff—a staff that transformed into a scythe. "Perhaps there's something in your eye."

Several detachable blades flicked out of the weapon. The stilettos struck each of the true loyalists in their faceplates, the red eyes acting like targets. From inside the chamber Davaros watched Morando's soldiers fall. The scythe-wielding warrior strode over to the core extractor and opened it. Davaros jumped out and hugged her savior, saying, "Thank you, Zadra."

Lieutenant Zadra removed the helmet, which she had "liberated" from the loyalists' weapons locker. But the trio of downed loyalists began to stir around them. Zadra once again donned the headpiece and said, "Thank me *if* we make it out of this citadel."

"Those loyalists," said Davaros as she and Zadra left the sector. "You didn't kill them!"

"I do show some restraint from time to time," Zadra deadpanned.

They took an ascensor to the top floor, then ran down a corridor. Multiple surveillance orbs lay inert on the floor. Davaros furrowed her brow and asked, "Did you do that?"

"Not directly," answered Zadra.

"Halt!" cried a voice behind them.

The three loyalists from Sector Black staggered out of another ascensor. They had removed their ruined helmets, revealing an assortment of angry alien faces.

"*They* deactivated the surveillance orbs!" said Davaros, ducking their Serrator blasts. "But I would have thought they'd sound a capture alarm instead."

"And say what, exactly?" asked Zadra, flicking more scythe blades. "That there's a traitor among their ranks? That three of Morando's deadliest soldiers were outwitted by a small girl?"

"Morando would send *them* to Sector Black!" Davaros realized.

"Correct," said Zadra. "For those three loyalists, their only chance of survival lies in apprehending you once again. At least, that's what I'm counting on. . . ."

The two rebels stole back into the communications sector, while the loyalists kept firing upon them. Unlike their last visit, Davaros noticed that the antechamber was empty.

"Where are the Blanks?" she asked.

"They've been recalled, following your 'break-in,'" said Zadra. "All of them will be inspected and reconditioned—except for this one."

The technology bay door retracted, revealing a lone Blank unit standing in front of the comms rig. Its sleek white body reflected in the panoramic windows beyond the servers. Zadra lowered the door again, hearing Serrators strike against the other side. Zadra addressed the robot.

"Blank unit, do you understand your new programming?" asked Zadra.

"Affirmative," said the robot.

The loyalists wrenched open the bay door at last and opened fire. But the Blank stepped in front of Zadra and Davaros. Serrator blasts ricocheted off its back like a standing shield.

Now covered by the Blank, Zadra struck her scythe against the glass wall behind them. The floor-to-ceiling window shattered outward. High-elevation winds howled into the room, and the loyalists stopped shooting so they could brace themselves. Zadra cinched Davaros's arms around her own waist and ordered, "Hold on to me. And your fear!"

She then took the Blank by the arm, and all three of them toppled out the broken window. The loyalists raced over and looked down. Zadra, Davaros, and the Blank fell together, plummeting rapidly toward lanes of swiftcycle traffic. Davaros shut her eyes, expecting to be struck by one of the flying vehicles—or to smash against the ground even farther below them.

Zadra began twirling the scythe with her free arm. Faster and faster the weapon spun, its phosphorescent blades blurring. Davaros cracked open one eye, realizing that their drop had slowed. She then saw Zadra's weapon circling over their heads like the rotors on a helicopter. Zadra gradually lowered them onto an idling swiftcycle, whose owner had stopped to watch the spectacle above him. The lieutenant pushed aside the dumbstruck driver, making room on his seat for herself, Davaros, and the Blank. She then slammed the swiftcycle's engines into full throttle, just as explosions shook the air around them. The Blank's free-floating head rotated and spotted the three loyalists jetting after them in a V-Stryker.

"They'll blow us out of the sky!" cried the Blank.

"Keep your head on," said Zadra. "While I get rid of mine."

She removed her stolen helmet and released it, letting the wind carry it directly into one of the V-Striker's intake vents. Everyone heard a loud crunch, and black smoke billowed out of the wing's exhaust port. The pursuit craft lost stability. With Zadra's true identity now exposed to the panicking loyalists, Davaros tried to pull the cowl over her lieutenant's face.

"Thank you, Davaros, but don't bother," said Zadra. "There's no turning back now."

She took the commandeered swiftcycle out of traffic and threaded between Akiridion-5's shimmering towers. The V-Striker chugged after, firing more plasma charges that thunderclapped around them. Zadra drove past traces of the destruction caused by Morando's coup—cratered streets and scorched buildings. But she also soared past signs of defiance, like glowing graffiti that said HOUSE TARRON LIVES!

Even though the V-Striker was down an engine, it still gained on the overcrowded swiftcycle. Davaros watched Morando's loyalists close the gap between them and said, "Should we off-load some unnecessary weight? Like the Blank or . . ."

She then looked at the swiftcycle owner. His eyes bugged as he understood her meaning.

"Definitely not the Blank," said Zadra, which did little to comfort the owner.

Another plasma charge went off under the swiftcycle, and its propulsion system failed. Zadra skidded the vehicle into a nearby neighborhood, then confirmed her fellow passengers were unharmed. A bright spotlight shone on the rebel party. Zadra shielded her eyes and looked up at the V-Striker looming above them, its rail guns deployed.

"You almost got us all the way back to Adronis Quadrant, Zadra," muttered Davaros.

"Close enough," said the lieutenant.

The block lit up as Serrators fired from the shadows, strafing the V-Striker. Davaros, the Blank, and the swiftcycle owner watched as Izita's Resistance fighters swarmed the enemy ship. Rebel soldiers cuffed the three loyalists in their cockpit before they could radio for reinforcements. Izita rushed over to Davaros and Zadra, saying, "You made it out alive. Praise Seklos."

"But without the comms array, Mother," said Davaros. "We failed the Resistance."

"That is one fear you needn't hold on to, Davaros," said Zadra.

The lieutenant elbowed the Blank unit beside her, knocking open its chest compartment—where the inner workings of Morando's comms rig remained safely smuggled. Zadra saluted the Blank and said, "Congratulations on following your new programming, soldier."

The Blank responded with an enthusiastic, "Yes, ma'am!"

Zadra then considered the swiftcycle owner, who had remained mute during their entire escape. With another salute she said, "Thank you for the use of your conveyance, citizen."

The Akiridion blinked, as if coming out of a state of shock, and said, "House Tarron lives!"

Zadra half smiled at the owner, hoping he was right—hoping that Aja and Krel could survive long enough for the Resistance to reach them with its brand-new comms array. . . . *This may turn out to be a great day after all*, Zadra thought.

CHAPTER 18

UNCONVENTIONAL METHODS

A peal of electrical feedback discharged from Aja the exact instant Foo-Foo's dagger struck her. The current coursed into the bounty hunter's suit, sending him flying. Krel ran over and held his motionless sister in his arms, residual electricity sparking between them.

"Aja!" he cried.

Luug trotted up to his owners. He released three Serrators and a hoverboard from his jaws, then whined when Aja wouldn't get up. Vex hobbled over, his face grim. He never, ever wanted to contemplate losing another member of House Tarron. Yet as Vex beheld Aja's still form, a smile broke across his face.

"Glorious!" he shouted.

Krel glowered, tears in his eyes, and said, "Vex! Can't you see my sister is—"

Aja's eyes blinked open. Krel yelled in surprise and dropped Aja. The back of her head bonked against the floor.

"Ow!" she groaned weakly. "Chill up, brother . . . or is it 'chill *out*'?'"

Vex and Krel burst into relieved laughter. Aja sat up and stared at the knife poking out of her chest. She tugged on the blade, and it came loose—with a skewered Pingpod stuck on the tip. It stabbed into, but not *through*, the ancient Akiridion accessory Aja had clipped to her shirt.

"A Pingpod!" said Vex. "Varvatos has not seen one in parsons. The electric pulse must have been triggered when the dagger pierced it. Princess Aja was merely stunned! That means—"

Vex cocked an eyebrow. He ambled over to the unmoving Foo-Foo, placed his ear against the smoking armor, and listened. A moment later he announced, "Varvatos Vex does not hear a heart-beat. The poor, darling, murderous creature. Varvatos will light a pyre and—"

Foo-Foo willed his heart to beat again and jolted

alive, and immediately began choking his former idol.

"Glor-*ack*-ous!" rasped Vex.

As he and Foo-Foo traded blows, the herd of Arcadia-Con attendees checked their phones and moved on. Most headed toward hall A, completely missing Aja's now-flickering appearance. With a flurry of pixels, her human disguise wore off, revealing Aja's Akiridion form. She covered herself with her four arms and exclaimed, "My transduction effect!"

"It must have short-circuited from the Pingpod feedback," Krel mused. "But it's not like anyone here will care. They don't even notice a geezer having a fistfight with a talking rabbit."

"But they will eventually," said Aja, still feeling exposed. "As their pop culture has shown us, there is only so much suspension of disbelief humans can tolerate. They will see through our ruse soon enough and realize that we and Foo-Foo are fact, not fiction."

"Fine," said Krel. "I suppose our 'secret identities' will be exposed the moment we use these in public."

"Actually, little brother," Aja said with a sly smile.

"I think I have a much better idea. . . ."

Krel looked at his sister. "Well? I'm waiting!" he said.

Most of Arcadia-Con's attendees squeezed into the darkened hall A, which was already filled to capacity. Team Trollhunters watched their struggle from a corner, where Claire had discretely teleported them. The move left her feeling feverish, so she now leaned against Jim. Beside them, Toby reunited with Nana, who had unknowingly acted as the emotional anchor for Claire's shadow-jump. They—along with Blinky, AAARRRGGHH!!!, and NotEnrique—all gazed in openmouthed awe at the *Gun Robot* panel, which was already in full swing.

"And that is why we built a practical, fully functioning Gun Robot for our close-ups," said the film's director, a stout, bearded man with a thick Mexican accent. "And for our fans!"

On cue, an animatronic Gun Robot walked onto the main stage, standing at an impressive thirty feet high. The hall erupted with claps, whistles, and camera flashes. Backstage, a team of special-effects artists manipulated Gun Robot's movements with handheld remotes—right beside Steve and Eli. The Creepslayerz jumped up and down in their free XXL *Gun Robot* T-shirts and gave two thumbs-up to the stage. Superagent Muldoon returned the gesture from the celebrity panel, then fielded another question from the audience.

"Why is it that Gun Robot fires upon the Laser Ninjas with his left hand in the latest trailer, when it's *clearly* established in part four that Gun Robot is programmed to be a *righty*?" asked a pale and indignant fan. "I mean, don't any of you care about your *own* mythology?"

"First of all, thanks for loving our work enough to notice the little details," said the actor. "Believe me, everybody up here cares. But we're only human. Well, except for the *big guy*!"

He jerked his thumb at the life-sized Gun Robot, which immediately stomped off the stage. The special-effects artists in the wings reacted with alarm, toggling levers on their unresponsive controls. Gun Robot smashed right through the nearest wall, plowing out of hall A and into the rest of the Convention Center. The audience applauded once more, even as the director yelled in Spanish at his baffled crew. At the back of the hall, Jim said, "Man, these promotional stunts are getting out of hand. Arcadia-Con's really fun, but also *exhausting*."

"The old Troll adage is true," added Blinky. "There *can* be too much of a good thing."

"I think I can make a shad—er, *shortcut*—to Nana's car now," said Claire.

"Buckle up," grumbled AAARRRGGHH!!!, dreading the drive home.

"Here, Nana, let me clean your glasses," Toby said, taking his grandmother's spectacles.

"Ooh, did someone turn out the lights?" Nana asked as Team Trollhunters escorted her into a brand-new black hole.

Varvatos Vex cackled with manic glee and pinned Foo-Foo between the prongs of his walking cane. But the Destroyer spring-kicked Vex away, then reclaimed his dagger. He hopped over to the prone Vex and held the blade high, its edge burning, until a shadow eclipsed it. Foo-Foo craned his head around and saw a colossal robot reaching for him.

"I am Gun Robot," squawked a synthesized voice. "And you have been a bad bunny."

Several aisles over, Krel and his outsider classmates laughed aloud. Were they back in school, the shy students might never have interacted. But at Arcadia-Con those very same teens seemed to open up, chitchatting with others and smiling more. It was as if they had finally relaxed, feeling more at ease in their element, more connected to other like-minded individuals—individuals like Krel.

They all huddled around his optimized cell phone, which streamed live video from Gun Robot's eye-cameras. Krel tapped his touch screen furiously, directing the automaton to grab Foo-Foo.

"Does everyone in your country have your hacking prowess?" asked one of the kids.

"Er, no," said Krel. "But I could not have assumed control of this Gun Robot without your collective knowledge of coding, short-wave frequencies, and dramatic entrance dialogue!"

The band of amateur hackers gave another wheezy cheer—which turned into a groan as Foo-Foo amputated Gun Robot's fingers with his hard-light dagger. Landing on his big feet, the bounty hunter bounced over to Vex, who still struggled to get up.

"If you won't choose to be my friend, I'll force you to be my friend," said Foo-Foo.

He was about to press his neural control discs onto Varvatos's neck, when a Serrator blast knocked off one of Foo-Foo's metal ears. Recoiling in surprise, Foo-Foo turned his lopsided head skyward. A flying figure circled above him. Attendees started to take notice of the airborne individual—and the enormous Gun Robot lumbering through Arcadia-Con.

"Look! Up in the rafters!"

"It's a girl!"

"It's a projection!"

"No, it's Sally-Go-Back!"

Aja smiled under a clear spherical helmet as the attendees went wild over her Sally-Go-Back costume. The pink fabric covered most of her blue skin, and the two extra arms folded behind her back. She fired more shots at Foo-Foo with her Serrator—which kind of resembled Sally's ray gun from a distance—and coasted along the ceiling on her hoverboard.

"This! Is! So! LIVELY!" Aja shouted with abandon.

"Sally" dive-bombed Foo-Foo, keeping him confined with another round of suppressive fire, then doubled back for another strike, skimming above the attendees' heads. Aja's electric blue eyes connected with the eyes of several young girls in the crowd, all of them wowed by the sight of their favorite adventurer in action. The princess felt her core swell with emotion. She realized that this pink-and-silver outfit was never intended to intimidate others. It was meant to inspire them to become their *own* heroes. Aja waved back to her fans, all too happy to act as a symbol for a whole new generation. And from the ground, a proud Varvatos Vex watched Aja take yet another step toward becoming her own warrior queen.

Landing in front of the gaming tables, Aja flushed out Foo-Foo. He sprinted away in the other direction, but was cut off by Gun Robot's remaining hand. Vex then blocked the only other escape route with his cane.

"Varvatos Vex applauds your capture of Foo-Foo," Vex said to his royals. "Although your methods in this comic convention are, well, *unconventional*."

"I am Foo-Foo the Destroyer!" Foo-Foo declared, as if he were convincing himself. "And I—"

The Arcadia-Con attendees all shouted loudly, "Awwwwwwwwww!"

"You won't find *this* quite so adorable!" the one-eared Foo-Foo shouted over them.

He opened the hatch on his armor. But this time, Foo-Foo retrieved a small object with a timer on its surface. Vex's eyes went wide, and he yelled, "Great Galen! It's a thermal incendiary!"

"Correct, Commander!" said Foo-Foo. "With a charge powerful enough to level this entire Earthling freak show!"

Aja and Vex exchanged a look of alarm with each other, and then with Krel, who now piloted Gun Robot from inside its hollow chest. While the Akiridions were distracted, Foo-Foo secretly shunted himself out of his own metal shell—just as he had done in the Oxiom galaxy. But unlike that dim intergalactic way station, the Convention Center's bright lights cast the *real* Foo-Foo in stark relief. He was not some proud and resilient rabbit-like creature. Instead he stood revealed as a frail and mewling little creature with rheumy, pitiless eyes. Battle scars lacerated his thin flesh. As he had done many times before, Foo-Foo the Destroyer was about to cheat death, when—

"ARF! ARF! ARF!" barked Luug.

The Corgi easily dwarfed the denuded Foo-Foo. The bounty hunter retreated back into his armor— only to realize too late what he had just done. He glared at the thermal incendiary in his suit's paw, its countdown clock reaching zero. There was no time left to stop the blast, so Aja decided their best option was to try containing it.

"One," she said, erecting a bubble shield around Foo-Foo with her Serrator.

"Two," Krel said from inside Gun Robot, his Serrator making a second bubble around Aja's.

"Three," Vex said as Aja created a third bubble with Vex's Serrator, which she'd held behind her back.

If Foo-Foo the Destroyer had any last words of his own, they were muted by the three-ply bubbles— and the blast from the thermal incendiary. All the Akiridions and Arcadia-Con attendees shielded their eyes as a pure, destructive force flashed and thundered within the combined bubble shields.

"Spectacular . . . ," Eli and Steve said together in the crowd.

"*Espectacular . . . ,*" said the *Gun Robot* director next to Steve and Eli.

Aja and Krel refused to let go of their Serrators, maintaining the three barriers for as long as they could. Then, just like that, the storm within stopped. The bubbles fizzled away one by one, releasing little more than a cloud of smoke. And some steaming bunny droppings.

"I always knew humans were strange, but this Arr-Kay-Dee-Ah Khan takes the Gorb," said the spirit of Deya the Deliverer.

"It is a peculiar ritual, I'll grant you that," conceded another former Trollhunter, Kanjigar the Courageous. "Yet it's also a showcase of humanity's greatest attribute—its imagination—and its potential for heroism."

The ghostly figures floated in the infinite afterlife known as the Void. They watched through a scrying window as Team Trollhunters drove away from the Convention Center. Nana's sedan sped recklessly down Main Street, and Deya said, "Fortunately, our current champions survived the experience. If only they survive the ride home. . . ."

Inside the car, Nana took a sharp left, making Jim, Claire, Toby, Blinky, and AAARRRGGHH!!! slide across their seats. NotEnrique opened the glove compartment from the inside and groused, "Oi! Watch those turns, lady!"

"I could've done without those three 'surprises' in the *Murder House* maze," Claire said. "But I gotta admit, the rest of the show was pretty cool!"

"Indeed!" Blinky enthused. "To see such depth and breadth of human interests . . . Why, this excursion was even more eventful than my last day out! Although I must say I was a tad underwhelmed by Detective Belaya. . . ."

"'Never meet your heroes,'" Nana quoted, "'because they're sure to disappoint you.'"

"Oh, I don't know about that," Jim said as he looked up at the sky. "I got to meet one of mine a couple of times, and he seemed like a pretty stand-up guy. In fact, it feels like he's always looking out for me. . . ."

Kanjigar smiled back at his young human successor through the scrying window and said, "It pleases me to no end that Jim Lake Jr. feels lightness in his heart now, for this respite shall be all too brief."

"Verily," intoned Deya. "Gunmar's mad bid for conquest continues, and the Eternal Night looms ever closer."

Steve and Eli exited the Convention Center, its doors now miraculously unlocked. Detective Scott and the Arcadia Oaks PD could never have guessed the disappearing barricades had anything to do with the implosion of a deranged, bounty-hunting bunny. Steve and Eli watched the detective hug his daughter, Darci, while a paramedic revived Mary with smelling salts.

"Mary, you won't believe what you missed!" said Shannon. "Arcadia-Con locked everyone inside! On purpose! Just so we could watch this rehearsed fight sequence! It's gotta be from an upcoming *Gun Robot* and *Sally-Go-Back* crossover! I didn't even know they were in the same cinematic universe!"

Hearing everything that happened while she was unconscious, Mary fainted again.

Steve shrugged and asked, "Do you think we'll ever know what really went on in there?"

"Highly unlikely," said Eli. "But suffice it to say, Creepers were *definitely* involved."

"Yo, Cosplayerz!" called Superagent Muldoon.

The actor poked his head out the back of a limousine, which pulled up in front of the Convention Center. He lowered his sunglasses and said, "We gotta do this again sometime! Have your guy call my guy. We'll do lunch!"

Superagent Muldoon made a C with his hand, and the limo drove into the sunset. Steve and Eli smiled and waved goodbye, their XXL *Earth Invaders* T-shirts fluttering in the breeze. Out of the corner of his mouth, Steve said, "Wait. Who's our guy?"

"I have no idea," Eli whispered back. "But bringing in a third Creepslayer might be a good thing. In case our collaboration ever breaks down again."

"Aw, c'mon, Eli!" said Steve. "We're a great team! We pulled out a win in the end!"

"*This* time," Eli said back. "But the only way I'm going to level up as a defender of the night is by not letting my feelings get so hurt anymore. It's just . . . When I commit to something, I go all-in, body and soul. You've known that about me, Steve—it's the Pepperjack way! But the downside of that commitment is that I sometimes take things way too personally. It'd be healthy for me to also do something else. My *own* thing. Like, I dunno, screenwriting . . ."

Steve placed his hand on Eli's shoulder and said, "Well, whatever you do, I know it's gonna be great, Pepperbuddy. And maybe I could try being a little more . . . uh, what do you call it when it's the opposite of pushing people away?"

"Inclusive?" said Eli.

"Yeah!" Steve said. "The Palchuk can try being a little more *inclusive*!"

"Oh, Steve!" Eli exclaimed.

He hugged his fellow Creepslayer, and Steve felt the sudden impulse to shove Eli into the nearest locker. But remembering his recent pledge, Steve instead leaned into the hug. He hoped he might spot Aja somewhere in the throngs of exiting attendees. Steve couldn't stop thinking about his run-in with her inside Arcadia-Con and had resolved to ask the angel-kicking ninja out on a date. But in light of his new, more inclusive approach, Steve wondered if it might be better to invite Aja to a "group thing" instead. . . .

Back in the Void, Deya shook her head at the embracing Creepslayerz and said, "Merlin only knows how these two misguided youths will ever reach their heroic destinies."

"Indeed," said Kanjigar. "Although I predict communication will be the key to the ascension of the Slayers of Creeps. Just as it will be for another whose fate is written in the stars."

He waved his transparent hand over the scrying window, and its perspective shifted not just across dimensions, but also time and space. The portal showed swirling nebulas, ringed planets, and violent supernovas before landing on the world known to its inhabitants as Akiridion-5. Deep inside the Resistance war room, Zadra, Izita, and Davaros watched rebel technicians install their stolen comms system. The holographic star charts expanded, thanks to the wider range of detection afforded by the new array. Their screens zoomed in on Pingpod's point of origin—until the signal abruptly disappeared.

"It went dead!" said Davaros.

Izita's eyes rounded with worry as she said, "If that Pingpod was, in fact, activated by our royals, then the Tarron children could be . . ."

The Resistance leader couldn't bear the thought. The rebels went silent, their expressions downcast. Zadra could feel their fear over the royals' survival, just as she felt her own. But that fear came coupled with another sensation, much to the lieutenant's surprise—hope.

"Do not give into dread, my sisters and brothers," said Zadra, addressing the war room. "Our Resistance will look back on this delson as a victory. For we now know the corner of the universe to which we must direct our outgoing messages. The next time we receive a signal from that region, we shall trace it back to Aja and Krel."

Galvanized by their lieutenant, the rebels redoubled their efforts, adjusting dials and scanning the cosmic airwaves. Izita squeezed Zadra's hand in appreciation. And with her free hand—the one that wore the ring of the Resistance—Zadra took up a communicator and said, "Prince and Princess Tarron, can you hear me? If you can hear me, there was a traitor on Akiridion-5. . . ."

"These tidings bode ill for the extraterrestrials exiled on the surface world," said Deya.

Her spirit then aimed the scrying window's mystical gaze on Aja, Krel, Varvatos, and Luug. They had just sneaked away from Gun Robot—its autonomous actions later deemed a malfunction by the special-effects artists—and returned the *Sally-Go-Back* wardrobe to the fashion exhibit right before the rest of their transduction effects evaporated. Now the royals, their bodyguard, and trustworthy pet rode in the back of Stuart's taco truck.

They all remained quiet during the voyage home, but for different reasons. Aja's mind replayed her stint as a high-flying superhero, loving how it felt to serve as an inspirational leader to others. Krel thought about his new, shy tech-savvy acquaintances and how they all promised to keep their little Gun Robot "joyride" a secret. Vex brooded over how close he came to losing the royals, wondering what King Fialkov and Queen Coranda would think of the soldier who betrayed them. And Luug was simply content to fill his drooling mandibles with bowl after bowl of ghost pepper salsa.

"Be that as it may, these Akiridions are resourceful renegades," said Kanjigar. "Though they do not realize it, the heirs of House Tarron have already aided our Trollhunters several times over in a single day. And they will do so again in the near future. But for now . . ."

Once more, the phantom Kanjigar swiped his

hand in front of the scrying window, fast-forwarding its view an hour into the future. Aja, Krel, Vex, and Luug joined Ricky and Lucy Blank on their living room couch. The ragtag assemblage of aliens, robots, and a sentient artificial intelligence all watched a *Gun Robot* marathon on their TV.

"This movie is a conceptual nightmare of klebtastic proportions!" Krel yelled at the screen. "Gun Robot's onboard polygraph detectors should see right through the demigod's lies!"

"Yes, little brother," Aja said patiently. "But as we now know, the plot hole is one of the many conventions of human entertainment."

"Speaking of conventions, Varvatos Vex swears to never attend another," said Vex. "Why, Varvatos would rather suffer a mauling in the jaws of a Durian Dung-Digester than set foot inside Arcadia-Con again!"

Mother said, "Commander, I have ordered the Mazes and Monsters game and thirteen-sided die you requested. It should arrive within two to three business delsons. With free shipping."

"Er, very good, Mother," Vex mumbled awkwardly in front of Aja and Krel. "It, ah, is for *research*! So that Varvatos might learn new ways to smite his who-man opponents in the chess park! Jerry and Phil shall suffer Varvatos's wrath!"

"It would seem that each of you enjoyed your time at this Arcadia-Con," Mother continued. "And not just because it was an excuse to avoid making repairs to my exterior."

Aja and Krel traded a sheepish look, and the queen-in-waiting said, "Please forgive us, Mother. We didn't mean to deceive you."

"For what it's worth, it did provide valuable insight into fringe human customs, after all," said the king-in-waiting.

"And a new respect for those who celebrate them," Aja added. "Yes, we went into the Arcadia-Con judging its attendees for 'geeking out' over such seemingly trivial things as fantasy films, comic books, and animated TV series."

"But now we see that many of these humans are merely lost souls," said Krel. "Souls who wish to find a safe place in an otherwise inhospitable universe via entertainment. In that sense maybe we are not so different. Maybe we are all 'aliens' deep down."

Aja nodded. "After the Arcadia-Con I felt closer to the humans than I have since we have been here on Earth," she said. "Maybe everyone wishes to be someone else once in a while. Humans cannot change forms. But they can put on costumes and makeup and be whoever they want for a short time. I can relate to that."

Aja and Krel smiled at each other, then went back to watching TV with Vex, Luug, the Blanks, and Mother. The window closed on the makeshift family, and Deya said, "These visitors from another world are just as surprising as their human counterparts."

"Yes," said Kanjigar with a knowing smile. "As the rightful heirs to the throne of Akiridion, Aja and Krel Tarron are possessed of an astounding nobility and grace. They are as kind as they are powerful. In many ways they remind me of their parents—and my dear friends—Fialkov and Coranda. Ah, but that is a tale for another time. . . ."

RICHARD ASHLEY HAMILTON is best known for his storytelling across DreamWorks Animation's How to Train Your Dragon franchise, having written for the Emmy-nominated *DreamWorks Dragons: Race to the Edge* on Netflix and the official DreamWorks Dragons expanded universe bible. In his heart, Richard remains a lifelong comic book fan and has written and developed numerous titles, including *Trollhunters: The Secret History of Trollkind* (with Marc Guggenheim) for Dark Horse Comics and his original series *Scoop* for Insight Editions. Richard lives in Silver Lake, California, with his wife and their two sons.